THE BOOK OF ALFAR

THE
BOOK
OF
ALFAR

A Tale of the Hudson Highlands

BY PETER W. HASSINGER

Illustrations by Brett Helquist

LAURA GERINGER BOOKS
An Imprint of HarperCollins*Publishers*

The Book of Alfar: A Tale of the Hudson Highlands

Text copyright © 2002 by Peter W. Hassinger

Illustrations copyright © 2002 by Brett Helquist

Library of Congress Cataloging-in-Publication Data

Hassinger, Peter.

  The book of Alfar: a tale of the Hudson Highlands / by Peter W. Hassinger; illustrations by Brett Helquist.

    p.   cm.

  Summary: In the legend-filled woods overlooking the Hudson River, an Algonquin girl is kidnapped by an evil dwarf whose grandson, aided by an eleven-year-old boy, a goatherd, and figures from the past, sets out to rescue her.

    ISBN 0-06-028469-2. — ISBN 0-06-028470-6 (lib. bdg.)

    [1. Supernatural—Fiction. 2. Dwarfs—Fiction. 3. Algonquin Indians—Fiction. 4. Indians of North America—Hudson River Valley (N.Y. and N.J.)—Fiction. 5. Kidnapping—Fiction. 6. Adventure and adventurers—Fiction. 7. Hudson River Falley (N.Y. and N.J.)—Fiction.] I. Helquist, Brett, ill. II. Title.

PZ7.H2788 Bo 2002   2001040902

[Fic]—dc21   CIP

                                                                AC

Typography by Alicia Mikles

1 2 3 4 5 6 7 8 9 10

First Edition

To

AVA, LAUREL, AND JESSE

THE BOOK OF ALFAR

Sander ran down the rocky path to Devil's Race, the creek behind the old stone farmhouse. The trail, barely visible beneath the brambly undergrowth, led to a line of trees bordered by an overgrown meadow gently pressed by the early-summer breeze. The grasses glinted in the bright sunlight and seemed, to Sander's eye, to move in a stately procession like a row of ships bending under sail. As he neared the water's edge, the trees grew thicker—oak, beech, and hornbeam hovering over the broad leaves of skunk cabbage that covered the slope. Sander stood on a rock catching his breath, tossed a strand of sandy hair out of his eyes, and, for a brief moment, envied the swirling water's clean getaway downstream.

The van that had transported the Schumerhorns' belongings was being unloaded piece by piece. He pictured his family like furniture bundled off the truck by burly moving men. Away came his mother, shaking with worry like a boxful of broken china. Away came his father, the great pontificator, bursting with big ideas like an overstuffed couch. Away came his teenage sister, sparking with anger like a lamp whose cord has frayed beyond repair, followed by Toby, with his insistent barking. Sander wanted no part of them. He inhaled the rich pine scent of the forest and moved upstream, toward the heart of Pyngyp Woods.

Slipping on a wet stone, Sander's feet plunged into the shallows. He moved gingerly around a rock outcropping where the dark clay bank had washed away to an old tree that straddled the stream. Toppled in storms long past, the tree rested on a massive semicircle of soil and gnarled roots like a slain warrior leaning crazily on his ancient shield.

The log seemed sturdy enough. Picking his way carefully, Sander gripped the thick, ropy twists of wood and clambered across to the remnant of a secluded trail leading up the mountain. He couldn't hear Toby's barking anymore. Maybe the dog had quit and curled up for a nap.

Sander worried his parents would notice he was missing. The sun was well over the hill by now, but he couldn't turn back. Curiosity drove him like a whip. A twig snapped about a hundred feet ahead, and he imagined it was a deer or a fox. Trying not to make a noise, he sped on, glancing into the woods on either side of the trail. He saw nothing. Then he heard a crunch—like a shoe on gravel.

Sander listened intently. Suddenly, through the trees, Sander spied a small boy wearing an old red baseball cap, walking hurriedly away from him with a stiff, jerky motion.

Sander ran after him and called for him to wait, but the boy didn't take any notice and, without changing his pace a bit, disappeared around a rocky bend.

Frustrated, Sander raced full tilt after him and crashed headlong into a wiry young girl coming from the opposite direction, carrying a small wicker basket. She sprawled across the path; a jumble of small cakes spilled alongside her.

"Are you all right?" Sander asked, helping the girl to her feet.

"You ruined my olykoeks," she exclaimed. The

girl was golden brown: brown skin, brown hair tied back, brown eyes, and a sprinkling of fine brown freckles like cinnamon across her face. She wore a pretty bead necklace. Sander liked her immediately.

He looked at the dozen little cakes strewn across the ground.

"I'm sorry," he said lamely.

"They were for you anyway."

"For me?" Sander looked at her quizzically.

"For your family. A welcome present," she said.

"Hey," he said, "what happened to that boy? You had to have seen him. I was chasing him along the trail. I'm surprised he didn't knock you down before I did."

"What did he look like?" she asked.

"He was about my height. Had a funny walk. Kinda jerky. Like one leg was longer than the other. And he was wearing an old baseball cap. Red, I think."

"An old baseball cap," she echoed. She gave him a long look. "Probably one of the local boys," she said slowly. "Maybe Bobby. He lives over on the other side of the mountain. He's a little shy if he doesn't know you. He takes care of the goats up on the hill. Part goat himself."

She knelt down on the trail and began picking the cakes up one by one. "Give me a hand," she said, looking up at Sander. He knelt beside her, and the two of them brushed the dirt off and packed the unbroken ones carefully back in the basket.

The girl rose and offered Sander her hand.

"I'm Mini," she said, smiling. "That's short for Minisceongo."

"That's a mouthful."

"It's Algonquin. That's why I use Mini."

"And I'm Sander," he said, coming to his feet alongside her. They shook hands, and she handed him the basket, turning away.

"Aren't you going to come home with me and meet everybody?" Sander asked.

"Another time," she said.

She stopped abruptly and put her head close to his. Her big brown eyes were open wide. He could feel her breath on his face. It smelled like fresh mint.

"Bring back the basket and meet me here tomorrow at first light. Whatever you do, remember, don't step off the trail." And then she was gone.

What a curious girl, Sander thought with a sigh. He hoisted the basket and headed back down the hill through Pyngyp Woods toward home.

CHAPTER TWO

The walls of the old abandoned mine rose up overhead, forming a cathedral of stone. Long, flickering shadows played across the ceiling like reflections through a stained-glass window. Granite pillars, shot through with blue-black magnetite, held the roof aloft. A pool of water flooded a large part of the floor.

A small, lone figure sat by a fire. He was a squat little man of indeterminate age, a dwarf, about three feet tall with a large head and long ears, creased leathery-brown skin, hairy eyebrows, and a long, pointy nose. He wore a red baseball cap, the brim just touching the dark, coarse hair that spilled out over his collar. Scrunched down in the dirt, hunched forward, legs crossed, he read from an old dog-eared Bible by the firelight and muttered to himself.

A harsh, raspy voice suddenly grated against the warm crackle of burning wood.

"Alfar, by King Goldmar, what the devil do you think you're doing?"

Alfar jumped up, startled. "Dwerg!"

Alfar looked around nervously but saw nothing. There was a rush of air from one pillar to the next. But Alfar could still see nothing except for a slight pinched spot, a quivering seam in the air.

"Look at you, for god's sake. Is that the Bible! Why do you insist on embarrassing yourself like this?"

"There's nobody to be embarrassed to," Alfar insisted.

"What am I, chopped liver?" the irritated voice complained. There was a ripple in the air in front of Alfar like waves of heat shimmering above flames, and an annoyed Dwerg appeared.

"I've been searching from Doodletown to Crickettown looking for you," Dwerg roared. "And here you are, hiding at Devil's Race." He had a thick, flowing beard and fierce, burning eyes like two glowing coals smoldering below his dark brow. He was on the tall side for a dwarf and an altogether imposing figure.

"Sorry, Granpa," Alfar squeaked out, abashed. "I left you a note," he added sheepishly.

"A note. I spend two hundred years of my life on you and all I get is a note. You should be ashamed of yourself for running away from home."

"But I've tried to tell you, Granpa, I don't want to be a Black Dwarf."

These words splashed on Dwerg like kerosene on a fire, and he flared up, larger than life. His giant shadow stretched to the upper reaches of the cavern, dark and menacing.

"Don't want to be a Black Dwarf?" He accentuated each word in a frightful whisper. "But you *are* a Black Dwarf. Of the Duergar," Dwerg insisted, then muttered in a quick undertone, "except on your mother's side." His voice rose again, becoming strident. "You don't *get* to choose. And you *will*"—he emphasized the *will* forcefully—"complete your education."

"But Granpa," Alfar protested.

Dwerg cut him off. "You are my lineage, a twenty-fifth-generation descendant of the great King Goldmar, and you had better start acting the part." Dwerg calmed down. His shadow shrunk from the ceiling.

"Look at this dump," he said, gesturing grandly

around the huge stone dome. "Your ancestral home is in the great cave at Dunderburg, in the Hall of the Mountain Lord. That's where you belong. Come home, Alfar. You owe it to your parents, your father."

"My father." Alfar's head came up.

"Rahbad," Dwerg repeated. "You dishonor his memory. He was a brave man. Have you forgotten?"

"Please, Grandfather," Alfar protested, trying to head off the inevitable. But Dwerg pressed on, as he always did.

"You must look again and see what kind of man your father was." Dwerg spoke sternly. He raised his arms and spread his cloak. Alfar flinched. Dwerg stood with arms outstretched. Nothing happened.

"Wake up," Dwerg spat out irritably, and the cloak stirred. It was inhabited by a wicked wight said to have once belonged to King Goldmar himself.

"Wait—I was in the middle of a dream," the wight protested.

"Get up," Dwerg said, snatching the cape off and hurling it into the air, where it hovered, disheveled.

"All right. All right," the wight said, ruffling his folds. "But I was working out something from my childhood."

"Later," Dwerg blustered. The wight shook

himself again and rose to a commanding height.

"Don't be afraid, my little Alfar," he crooned. "So many nights I have sung to you. Don't you remember? And now, my sleepykins, an old and familiar tale."

With an ominous rush, the cloak soared into the air above the fire. It hung there and seemed to gather the firelight into its undulating folds. Then it dove into the pool of water by Alfar's feet.

An image took shape on the surface of the water: High above a river, in the Highland wilderness, a rude cabin pressed against Dunderburg's mountain wall. Alfar watched helplessly. Before his mesmerized gaze, Alfar's father chopped wood. His mother tended a small garden. "It was before I found the great cave," Dwerg recounted. "We had been in the Highlands only six months. You were an infant, born on the crossing. I was out hunting when the Algonquin came from the south."

Alfar saw several Indians run into the clearing near where his father was working. His father picked up his musket and fired, and one Indian fell. The second kept coming, tomahawk raised. Rahbad struck him a blow with the butt of the musket, and he also fell. Alfar's mother was shrieking, and Rahbad gestured for her to run inside the cabin.

"Your father's only thought was to save you and your mother," Dwerg continued.

A third Indian reached Rahbad and struck his raised arm, drawing blood. Rahbad fell, arms flailing, during the struggle with several braves. His mother barred the door and hurriedly picked up the sleeping Alfar. She hid with him in a root cellar dug out below the wall of stone at the rear of the cabin. A flaming arrow caught the roof outside.

A smoky haze momentarily obscured the vision floating on the pool of water. Then Alfar saw his grandfather emerge from the forest, dropping his game bag in horror at the sight of the smoldering ruin. His mother emerged from the safety of the root cellar, cradling Alfar in her arms.

"I could have saved Rahbad with my knowledge of the sacred teachings," Dwerg went on. "But I was too late."

There was a whoosh as the image of the scene seemed to be sucked from the surface of the pool into the air of the cavern, leaving the water boiling in its wake. Alfar gasped. The fire flared back up. The wight hung in the air and shook off the water like a wet dog.

"Darn, that's cold," the wight said, then flew back onto Dwerg's shoulders.

"Your father never had the opportunity to complete his training," Dwerg said with finality, "but I swore I would not repeat that mistake with you."

"All right, Granpa, what would you have me do?" Alfar said, defeated.

"Make mischief, my boy, make mischief. Maybe this old mine isn't such a bad idea after all. You can work here, then return to Dunderburg when you're ready.

"There's a new family moved into the deKuyper house. You can practice on them. Yes, stay in your little hovel for the time being. It's homey and has a nice scent of sulfur. But for god's sake get rid of that Bible. It gives me the creeps."

"I like the stories," Alfar said.

"Just get it out of my sight," Dwerg finished, cutting him off. Alfar swiftly stuck the Bible into his waistband behind his back. He held his empty arms in front of him for Dwerg to see.

"Poof. Gone. Okay?"

"Okay," Dwerg responded. Then, in a conciliatory gesture, he reached into his cloak and drew out a shiny metal girdle.

"I almost forgot." Dwerg presented his grandson with a beautiful hand-wrought silver belt with delicate scrollwork engraved on its bright metal scales. He handed it to Alfar. "Try this on," Dwerg said. "It's called Silverstorm. The design is Scythian. But the magic is pure Black Dwarf."

Alfar reached for Silverstorm and felt its heft. The belt was amazingly light. The scales were thin as the first skin of ice on a winter's pond, but very strong. He ran his fingers over the intricate tracery that covered the surface.

Dwerg broke into his thoughts. "You'd better practice around the house before you try it. Invisibility takes a little getting used to. You don't quite know where your body is at first."

"I don't know what to say, Granpa," Alfar said.

"'Thank you' works for me," replied Dwerg.

"Thank you," Alfar answered dutifully.

"Now I must be going," Dwerg announced. He grasped his cloak and wrapped it around him.

"Where to, boss?" the wight said.

"The Great Hall, wight," Dwerg answered.

There was a furious motion and the sound of beating wings, and Alfar watched a screech owl flap his way over his head. The owl spoke.

"And don't forget to practice your shape-shifting, too," Dwerg said. "Remember, Alfar, you are of a proud and ancient lineage. The future generations of Black Dwarfs are counting on you. I've spent hundreds of years building a reputation in the New World. My name and works must be carried forward, and with your father gone . . . it's all up to you!"

"Could we stop for a field mouse or something? I'm feeling a bit peckish," the wight said.

"Fly," roared Dwerg.

The owl circled briefly, then headed up the tunnel of Devil's Race toward the surface. A piercing cry hung in the air after he was gone.

CHAPTER THREE

Sander's absence had barely been noted. He saw stacked up on the screened porch the pile of flattened cardboard cartons that had held the Schumerhorns' belongings. He banged the screen door closed behind him and set the basket of olykoeks on the antique oaken table. He could hear his sister and mother upstairs.

He found his father in the parlor. A big, bearish, bespectacled man, he sat reading on the floor next to several boxes of books. His arm rested on one half emptied, beneath a wall of partially filled shelves. He looked up distractedly at his son.

"What's for dinner?" Sander asked, his stomach growling.

"Dunno," his father answered, and unpacked

another book. "Look, my old star guide. What do you say we get the telescope out later and see what kind of sky we've got up here in the Highlands? The moon'll be full soon, but we should still have plenty of dark. No more streetlights. Wha'd'ya say?"

"Sure. Sagittarius should be visible about ten thirty."

Dinner was late. Mom heated up leftover samp porridge, a colonial meal of meat and vegetables that simmered for days until it turned into a thick, crusty, chunky paste. She said it traveled well, so it had been their last meal at their old house the night before. Sander hadn't liked it any better the first time. His mother served the horrid stuff up in heaping ladlefuls from a pot on the table. Her free hand swept back wisps of deep-red hair from her forehead as she dipped a too-generous dollop onto Sander's plate. He grimaced.

Sander's sister had an angry expression on her face, but it wasn't about the food.

"Not a tour," she complained loudly. "I'll move out if you do that, Mom, I swear."

"We'll open only on weekends, Colby, once the house is ready," her mother countered. "Just think.

You'd be living in a house listed in the National Registry! How many kids can say that?"

"How many would want to?" her daughter answered, frowning. Once she had dreamed of being a star at her old high school. Now her mother's dream had bowled hers over like a wrecking ball.

"Oh, Colby, it's not so bad," Sander's father said, playing peacemaker. "And anyway, we can keep your room off-limits. Can't we?" He looked to his wife for confirmation. None was forthcoming.

"I'm not sure I want to give her that," Mom responded, pausing a beat and drawing it out before adding weightily, "yet."

Colby rose abruptly, her chair scraping against the stone floor. "Don't hold me hostage, okay, Ma?" she said, exasperated, and threw down her napkin. She stalked out of the room.

"Colby, don't walk away from me. I need you to stay in the conversation," her mother called after her. Sander rolled his eyes. Colby could be heard stomping up the stairs to her room.

"Why does this always happen at dinner? It's bad for the digestion," Dad observed wryly.

"You think I should have waited to tell her?" Sander's mom asked, irritated. "It's not as if we haven't been planning and discussing this move for the past six months."

"She needs time to get used to living in the country," his father replied. "It's going to take a while before she makes new friends."

Sander started to get nervous. He hated disagreement.

He held out the basket with Mini's gift. "Oilycakes," he said, grateful for the chance to change the subject.

His father and mother each took one, smiling. Sander breathed a sigh of relief.

The farmhouse stood on the crest of a low rise of meadow above Devil's Race opposite the tall-standing firs of Pyngyp. The sandstone house was built in the style of the pre–Revolutionary War era—long and low and topped with a graceful double-gambrel roof in the Dutch manner. The dark slate shingling of the roof shone in the starlight through the sheltering overhang of a large red maple.

Sander looked out into the purpling darkness and listened to the rhythmic chirping of the crickets as his dad adjusted the legs of the tripod. Sagittarius appeared low over the southern horizon.

"How are *you* doing with this move?" Sander's father asked.

"Okay, I guess," Sander replied. Then, after thinking for a moment, "How about you?"

His father laughed. "Okay, I guess. This is a land of legend, after all. There's plenty of history to keep me happy."

"What is it about the past that you like so much, Dad?" Sander asked.

"It's not the past for me, son. Some people think time is like a corridor—you look back down to see things that don't mean anything anymore. For me, the past fills the present. It exists simultaneously, side by side. And when it speaks to you, it isn't in the voice of a ghost. It's alive. And it has something important to tell us. If we listen."

"Like what?" Sander asked.

"You've got to poke around to find out. These hills, for instance, used to be a hideout for all sorts of desperate people. Runaways, thieves, Indian families, escaped slaves, deserters. One died not far from here, up Pyngyp Mountain in fact. The place is steeped in old lore and ancient spirits."

"What does that have to do with us?" Sander asked.

"For me, maybe nothing. For you? That's for you to find out."

His father aimed the telescope and stepped back. "Here, take a look."

Sander could make out the rough outlines of the teapot in the southern sky and the dark shadow that marked the Lagoon Nebula. Sagittarius.

"Did you know that when Virgil and Dante wrote their poems, they put centaurs at the gates to the underworld to represent Sagittarius?" Sander's father asked.

"Why Sagittarius?" Sander asked.

"Our planet's path crosses the Milky Way between Scorpio and Sagittarius. And the ancients believed that that intersection was the gateway to the after-life—the road traveled by the souls of the dead."

"I'm not seeing any souls, just stars," said Sander, giving an exaggerated squint.

"Just keep looking, Sander, keep looking," his father said.

A bright globe of a moon surfaced in the sapphire-blue sky. Sander turned over in his bed, dreaming.

Alfar crossed the kill, Silverstorm about his waist. He stood stock-still in the grasses, waiting.

The evening air brought sweet smells to his sharpened senses. He passed an hour lost in thought.

When the moon hung low above the trees like a fat white marble glowing with reflected light, Alfar moved up close to the farmhouse. There was something reassuring about its great age, as the growing shadows from the moonlight seemed to take it deeper into darkness.

Alfar knew before he even crossed the creek that there was a dog. He circled around the shed next to the big barn in back of the house, stopping near the old rabbit hutch with its torn screening and wooden door hanging by a rusted hinge.

At that moment, disturbed by a dream, Sander awoke and climbed out of bed. He went over to the window. Peering into the twilight, he thought he saw a small figure moving out by the barns. He was suddenly wide-awake. He watched the shadows intently.

Alfar took a few steps out into the open. As far as he could tell, the dog was shut in on the porch. The coast was clear. Still, he couldn't be too sure. A dog bite was a nasty business. Mustering his courage, Alfar reached down and took hold of Silverstorm. In a single swift move he turned it from back to front. Instantly, he vanished.

Sander stood openmouthed at the window above the yard. A moment later an aluminum folding chair toppled over mid yard as if struck by an unseen hand. There was a thud, followed by a sudden commotion. The chair seemed to pick itself up and fly away into the darkness.

From his resting spot on the back porch below, Toby erupted into a torrent of sharp barking. Sander thought he saw a shadow moving along the grass toward the garbage. But he couldn't be sure. Alfar, furious at himself for tripping over the chair, ignored the dog and ran quickly toward the garbage can. He knew he had to work quickly.

He reached for the handle and gave it a yank upward, but the can only tottered and the lid didn't budge. He gave another big yank, and the handle came free. The big can tipped over, spilling wet garbage all over. Alfar slipped and fell a second time, rolling in the trash. Annoyed at his clumsiness, he was momentarily blinded by a yellow shaft of a light sweeping over the scene.

"Hey," Sander's father said, seeing the tipped can. "Get away from there!" The flashlight stabbed into the darkness.

Fearing the dog, Alfar took off as fast as his invisible little legs could carry him.

Toby barked some more, but Sander's father wasn't about to let Toby get bitten by a hungry raccoon. He shushed Toby, giving him a congratulatory scratch on the back of the neck for his superior watchdog skills. All was quiet, except for one last crash as the retreating Alfar tripped again over the aluminum folding chair that he had hurled in his fit of pique moments before.

Upstairs, Sander stared at the darkened yard. There, for the briefest of moments, he had seen a ragged little man wearing a red baseball cap—a dwarf, plain as day. And then, in a twinkling, he had disappeared.

CHAPTER FOUR

The next morning Sander was up before anyone else. He methodically searched the backyard for some sign of the previous night's visitor. After a half hour he was rewarded with the discovery of a good set of child-sized footprints slightly smaller than his own. They were in a sandy area near the shed by the old rabbit hutch. He had seen the little man standing there just before he had disappeared.

Sander was thrilled at the confirmation and bursting to tell someone, only he couldn't think of a soul who would believe him. All his old friends were miles and miles away. Then he remembered Mini. He was supposed to meet her on the mountain at first light!

Sander led the way while Toby sniffed along

behind him. In no time at all they reached the bend with the rocky outcropping where he had run into Mini the day before. The boy and his dog halted briefly, then continued along the trail.

The path grew steeper and narrower as he traversed the mountain's flank. Above, Sander thought he saw goats negotiating the stony slope. Below, he heard the rushing of the creek. He could make out a ruin in the water. His father had told him that there used to be an old icehouse near the farm. Huge, caved-in beams were piled in a blackened jumble where the stream broadened, turned, and rushed foaming against a rocky shelf before joining Tiorati Brook below Devil's Race.

Sander looked around for Toby, calling for the dog, but there was no response. He must have wandered off the trail. The longer he waited, the harder Toby might be to find. Then he heard a crashing sound in the brush above him. Forgetting all about Mini's warning, he set the basket down and stepped off the trail into the thick undergrowth, following the direction of the sound.

After a few steps he looked over his shoulder, but the trail was already invisible. He tried to find a landmark he had noted—a tall pine with a lightning breach down its side. But the blasted pine, like the dog, was nowhere to be seen. In fact, the forest itself seemed different, sunnier, the leaves greener; and the canopy smaller than it had been, he imagined, only moments before. The trees seemed younger and not as tall as they had appeared from the trail. Sander shivered.

Sander took out his Cub Scout knife and carefully marked the trees as he moved deeper into the forest. That way, he figured, he could always find his way back to the trail. After a fruitless half hour he thought he heard a sound off in the distance. For a moment he thought maybe it was Mini. He imagined that she had found Toby and was looking for him. But why would she be running? he wondered.

He started back in the direction of the trail but stopped abruptly. He was sure now that he heard footsteps. They were moving rapidly, and they were heading his way, crashing heavily through the brush. On instinct Sander ducked under heavy foliage and hid.

Peering out, he saw a soldier of about nineteen or twenty running toward him as fast as he could go. He wore a threadbare and bedraggled uniform that had once been bright blue. He carried no weapon.

He passed so close to Sander's hiding place that the boy could clearly see his eyes. They were filled with terror. He took no notice of Sander. Suddenly the bushes next to Sander shook. A painted Indian warrior leaped past, tomahawk in hand. A bright feather was tied to the handle of his tomahawk.

The brave was not alone. Sander could make out two or three others in a line stretching out through the trees. They were like a pack of wolves running down their victim. After they had gone, Sander was afraid to move. He sat there for what seemed like forever. He wanted only one thing: to go home.

Sander headed down the hill as fast as he could go. He pushed through the brush and stepped out at last onto the open trail. He stumbled over the missing Toby, who was nosing in the bushes along the path. Toby gave him a sniff and a lick.

"Sander!" He heard Mini's voice cry out from nearby. "Where have you been?" Sander rolled to his feet and dusted himself off as Toby panted around his legs. Mini ran up to him, holding the basket.

He grabbed her by the arm and started to drag her back down the hill.

"Shhh—quiet or they'll hear you," he whispered fiercely in her ear.

"What are you talking about?" she said, struggling out of his grasp.

"Indians. I saw Indians. They were this close," he said spreading his hands apart a few inches to demonstrate. "And they were chasing some guy with their tomahawks," Sander continued breathlessly, frightened.

"You're seeing things," said Mini. "I warned you about going off the trail."

"Keep your voice down. They passed this way minutes ago, and they may come back any second," Sander pleaded. "Mini, that man I saw is going to die. I know it. I felt it. He was a soldier, like from the time of the Revolution. But not one of ours and not British, either. He ran right past me, scared out of his wits."

Mini gave him a piercing look. "Sounds like you saw a ghost," she said. "Come with me. I want to show you something."

The sun was high and the air was hot and sticky, but Sander didn't mind. As he and Toby made their way over the rough, uneven surface, Mini pointed out the sights. The ruins of the old icehouse by the water could be clearly seen from Goat's Walk. Below the swath of stone, she indicated the remains of a tumbledown old shed set back in among a few scrawny trees. The shed was abandoned now, except for mice and birds.

Sander missed his footing and kicked a stone, causing a slight slide of smaller stones and pebbles, which skidded down and disappeared over a rocky shelf projecting out above the creek.

"This way," Mini directed him, veering off to the right, away from the danger.

Mini moved surefootedly across the scrabble slope to an opening in the trees, where the trail picked up once again.

Sander, relieved to be off the unstable slope of Goat's Walk, described the strange visit of the little man the night before. He finished with a question.

"When you ran off yesterday, you knew it wasn't Bobby I saw, didn't you?"

"Turned out that Bobby was on the north side all day," Mini answered. "I've never heard any stories about a dwarf in these woods. But there's an old legend about a dwarf who's the Lord of Dunderburg Mountain. That's the big mountain to the north above the river. Here's the gorge," she added, leading him onto a flat stone ledge. "Afraid of heights?"

The air stirred, and Mini stepped out farther onto

the open surface of Pyngyp's stone roof, golden in the afternoon sun. The clouds floated by like stately flat-bottomed boats sailing along the Hudson.

"Legend has it that a Hessian soldier died up here during the American Revolution," she said. "He was a deserter."

"So that was who I saw today. It must've been just before . . ." Sander let the thought trail off.

Mini walked out as close to the edge as she dared.

"The soldier leaped to his death from this cliff. It's called Hessian Falls."

Sander watched a butterfly rise up and float just out of reach in the empty space above the stony amphitheater below. "We're at the top of the world," he whispered. Toby lay down panting at his feet.

"That's the real top. Dunderburg. Over there," said Mini, pointing toward a large, dark, craggy shape hunched above a bend in the river. "That's where the dwarf is supposed to live." Mini stared out at the large, forbidding mountain. "He's sent storms to sink ships trying to make it through the narrows. Sailors used to dip their sails in his honor to keep from being blown over."

"I don't think this was him. This dwarf couldn't even tip over a trash can."

At the foot of Hessian Falls, shards of slatelike stone covered the ground like broken crockery where the cliff face had sheared off eons ago and smashed into a million pieces. A cracked shelf ran along the base of the cliff wall. The only smooth patch of ground lay in the shelter of a single old hawthorn tree almost thirty feet tall that stood beneath the cliff and seemed to preside over the otherwise empty clearing.

The larger boulders shielded the hawthorn from the smothering press of coniferous trees that dominated the hillside below. Its myriad branches were dotted with white, pink, and brown flowers that surrounded the scarlet fruit of the haw.

Sander and Mini slipped through a rocky cleft into the amphitheater. Sander pushed past Mini and raced excitedly across the floor of the enclosure and toward the lip of stone at the base of the cliff. He tripped over a rock outcropping and fell. Mini hurried over to see if Sander was all right.

"It's just a little cut," Sander said, wincing slightly. He held his bony knee; the ripped pant leg showed the raw skin with the blood slowly dripping out from a series of dark, irregular lines packed with dirt.

Mini pulled a wrinkled Kleenex out of her pocket and dabbed the bruise.

"We better get going," she said.

Sander got to his feet, and as he did so, a dull glint from the sandy earth caught his eye. He reached back down and scraped at the surface.

"Hey, Mini. Look at this," he said.

A rusted metal wedge and then a rectangular shape emerged beneath Sander's hand. He got a grip on it and worked it free. He held it up for Mini to inspect. It was a small oblong metal tin with a monogram he couldn't read and the embossed figure of a lion, glowing in the afternoon sun.

"Now what the heck do you suppose this is?" Sander asked. He shook the tin, and it rattled.

"It's got a pebble in it." He tried to open the tin, but it was weathered shut.

In the parlor Sander's father turned the tin over carefully in his hand, examining it under a magnifying glass. He thumbed through a volume with pictures of badges and coats of arms. Sander watched him and thought of all the things he *wasn't* telling his father, about the little man and the ghost and the legend of the Lord of the Dunderburg. His father looked up.

"This is the real thing, Sander, a tinderbox. This lion is a Hessian symbol, and the monogram is for the Count of Landgrave, none other than Frederick the Second, King of Prussia at the time of the Revolutionary War."

Sander felt a thrill go up his spine.

"But what is it for?"

"It's a matchbox. Hessian soldiers—grenadiers—wore them on their belts, and in the old days they held lit fuses to set off weapons and explosives."

His father handed the tin back to him.

"What are you going to do with it?" his father asked.

"I don't know. Keep it in my room, I guess," Sander replied.

His father nodded thoughtfully, eyeing him closely.

"His name was Herder. Josef Herder. He was a conscript, a nineteen-year-old boy who came to America to fight for the British against the colonists. He was very poor. He came from a family of turf cutters, harvesting peat from bogs in northwest Germany to sell for making fires. But he wasn't cut out to be a soldier. So he deserted in the heat of battle and made his way north to the Ramapoughs."

"How do you know all this?"

"I was talking to someone at the local historical society."

"Why did he jump?"

His father's eyebrows went up. "So you know the story?"

"A little," Sander replied. "Mini told me."

"No one really knows why he jumped," his father continued. "The legend is that he was being chased by Indians and afraid of being captured and tortured, so he took his own life."

"So you think this box came from his belt?" Sander asked.

"Looks like. It fits the story," his father said. "I wonder why it's been unearthed now?"

"What do you mean? I found it."

"Yes. You found it. But it's been lying there for almost two hundred years. Funny that it pops out today. Into your hands. What do you think is in it?"

Sander rattled the tin again. "A stone or something," he answered.

"Let me see it," his father said, as Sander handed the tin back to him.

His father fiddled with the catch for a minute.

He took out his pocketknife and worried the clasp.

"Don't break it," Sander said, suddenly anxious.

It came loose and his father handed it right back to Sander without looking inside. Sander shook the pebble onto his open palm.

It wasn't a pebble at all. It was some kind of small piece of grooved bone that had been hollowed out, with a carved design and colored with the faded remnants of what once might have been red paint.

Sander held it out so his father could see. He put the magnifying glass over it.

"Why, it's a bead," he said.

"I wonder how it got there," Sander said.

"I'm sure it meant something to Herder. Like a good-luck charm or something."

"Didn't do *him* much good," Sander observed.

"Well, it's yours now," his father said.

CHAPTER FIVE

The meadow grass was rife with fiddlehead, milkweed, and wild asparagus. Along its perimeter, a thicket of greenbrier and hawthorn had insinuated itself, spilling out from the woods into the aging pasture. An intricate lacing of vines linked the insurgent clumps. A stand of young black birch stood poised to break out of the thicket into the remaining open ground, biding its time with the ancient patience of the forest. A nuthatch sounded its low nasal call. The notes came in rapid succession.

Sidling his way through the field, Alfar saw what he was looking for: the flowers of a low, sprawling shrub, the leaf stalks set in a thorny base. He tugged at his baseball cap. Then, reaching for the swelling, purple fruit, he plucked it and popped the gooseberry into his mouth. The juice ran from the corner of his mouth down his chin. He savored the sweet taste, and then his fingers ran quickly over the plant, grabbing the berries. Alfar grazed, filling a small leather sack as he ate.

A bee was perched on a petal, foraging for nectar. Alfar watched as it drank deeply, slowly detached itself from the flower, and spiraled upward. Alfar dreamily imagined it headed back to the hive.

Instead, the bee suddenly rushed to a spot about six inches in front of Alfar's face, right between his eyes. It hung there, hovering, and Dwerg's raspy voice buzzed at him. "What the devil do you think you're doing?"

"Grandfather!" Alfar took a step backward in surprise, coughing up a gooseberry. He quickly rubbed the trickle of juice from his chin.

There was a rush of air as the bee grew large; the wind from his wings flattened the grass and almost knocked Alfar over. Then the bee exploded into the whirling, shapeless mass of Dwerg's dark cloak, and his grandfather, the Lord of the Dunderburg, stood before him, arms folded, glaring at Alfar with a critical eye.

"Why, gooseberries, Granpa. I was just eating some gooseberries."

"Not the gooseberries, boy. The mischief. What happened to the mischief?"

Alfar fumbled for an explanation. "Well, I had a little trouble with the belt."

"Trouble," Dwerg snorted. "I'll say. I saw the whole fiasco from the barn. You're centuries old, for crying out loud. When are you going to grow up?"

Alfar stared at the ground and shuffled his feet. "I'm sorry, Granpa," he offered. "I'll try and do better next time."

"All right. You've got to get right back on the horse. You need to practice your invisibility. I told you to try it at home first. You'll get used to it. But right now I've got something else in mind." His grandfather pulled himself up to his full height. "Put down those gooseberries and let's get to work."

"Okay," Alfar agreed resignedly, and rolled his eyes.

From across the field, the two figures were barely discernible standing amidst the branches of a fallen black locust at the far side of the pasture. A victim of an ice storm the previous winter, the locust had valiantly produced a few leaves and drooping clusters of white flowers. But it was clear this would be its last year.

Alfar watched a honey-laden worker bee pass under the shallow leafy covering and disappear against the deep ridges of dark-gray bark.

"Easy now," Dwerg cautioned. "Remember what I told you."

The hive was brimming with hundreds of bees. Alfar took a deep breath and snatched it up. With a single stroke he cracked it open cleanly on the trunk of the locust. A thick, angry cloud of bees rose into the air, circling around Alfar.

"Hurry," Dwerg urged him.

Alfar searched the open honeycomb swiftly, disregarding drones, workers, and larvae in various stages of transformation. His eyes widened. He spied the queen. Her size alone marked her as different from the rest. He plucked the queen as if she were a gooseberry and slipped a horsehair loop over her waist. The angry droning rose to a roar. He tightened the loop gently, so as not to injure her abdomen. With the end of the loop woven into a long filament tied to his belt, he released the queen. He tossed her into the air and let her run out the length of lariat.

It was at that moment that the bees attacked. His

thick, leathery skin gave him some protection, but it was not enough.

"Ow," said Alfar, swatting, his baseball cap held in his free hand. "Ow. Ow."

"Hang on, boy," his grandfather said, cheering him on from a safe distance. "You've got her now. They'll start to swarm in a minute."

The queen fluttered for an instant, dipping toward the ground. Then, finding new strength, she rose to a commanding height ten feet above the fallen locust tree. The cloud of angry bees surrounding Alfar suddenly stopped their attack and, sensing their queen, streamed toward her. The queen made for a low branch of the nearest bush, close to the ground only a few yards away. The bees followed. Within seconds, she was covered with a writhing mass of bees as thick as a man's fist.

"All right, Alfar. That's it. Go, go. Get the skep."

Alfar, aching with bee stings, snatched the hiving skep, a wooden box with a long handle for snagging the bees. He held it under the swarm and shook the bees into it. He closed it and the job was done. He sat down heavily and took a deep breath. Dwerg came close, looked down on him, and shook his head.

"Tsk, tsk, tsk. They sure made a mess of your face."

Alfar looked up at him. His face and arms were a mass of lumpy, red, swollen tissue.

"Don't worry, Alfar. Revenge heals all wounds. I promise you that."

"I don't know if I can wait that long," Alfar answered plaintively.

"All right. Come with me over to the other pasture. It's got horses. I'll make you a poultice to take the swelling down and draw the fire out of those stings."

"What poultice?"

"Nettles and horse pee," Dwerg replied, and marched off. Alfar wrinkled his nose, rose, and tottered after his grandfather, carrying the skep humming with bees.

It was the middle of the night when a light rustling from inside the plaster wall alongside his bed woke Sander. There was a small closet at the foot of his bed and a little door at the back that led to a crawl space that connected to the attic. There, on top of the wooden slats with the plaster lathing, was where his mom had packed away the family's winter clothes waiting for the cool fall weather.

He lay still, trying to decide if there was a mouse working its way along inside the wall.

The squirrel was fat, gray, and fluffy, with cheeks full of acorns. He moved across the lathing slowly. His eyes squinted into the dark, head nervously twitching from side to side. He spit out an acorn and muttered to himself.

"Darn pouch mouths. How do they stand these acorns?"

The acorn bounced and rattled lightly off into the darkness. Alfar grumbled and moved on. He searched for a spot not far from the hole under the eaves where he had squeezed his way into the old farmhouse attic. Only the tiny leather pouch around his neck suggested that he was more than just a poor animal looking for a comfortable place to lay his head on a cool summer's night.

Alfar began scratching at the plaster with his front paws. He made a hole between the wooden slats and exposed a hollow space inside, roughly the height of the beam. He sat up straight and looked around the attic, as if to make sure no one was watching. With his paws gently holding the leather sack around his neck so to protect the contents, he worried open the little bag with his teeth.

"Shape-shifting, revenge . . . what a silly business."

Ever so carefully Alfar tipped the bag over and dumped a small section of honeycomb, with the queen bee, out onto the wooden slat. With his nose he pushed the honeycomb section into the hole he had made in the space above the parlor ceiling.

His work complete, the squirrel wheeled abruptly to retrace his steps back toward the eave where he had made his entrance. He imagined the brief run across the open shingled roof; the leap onto the long, lowering tree limb on the north side of the house, leading to the trunk; and the scramble to safety back on the ground.

But on his way out, he took a wrong turn through the cardboard boxes filled with Sander's winter clothes.

He moved along the beam in the dark, planning to follow it to the end where it would meet the path he had taken on the way in. Worrying about what getting lost would do to his plan, he failed to notice the thin, wispy film that filled the angle between the beam and the upright. He walked right into the cobweb, tearing a section loose from its footings.

In the web's upper reaches the house spider stirred at the shock waves traveling along the fine strands. Looking down to see what it had caught, it found a most unlikely prey. A large squirrel stood stock-still. Its breaths came in short fast heaves. The lower section of web was draped over its head like a cloak; the animal was paralyzed with fear.

Attercop! Alfar forced the thought back into the dim recesses of his squirrel brain. Once, when he was young, Grandfather Dwerg had led Alfar through a garden at dawn after a night of mischief. Alfar had accidentally stumbled into the dew-spattered curtain of a garden spider stretched between two tomato plants. Alfar had felt the fine filament of the web cover his face and found himself gasping for air. The spiraling threads seemed to cling to his skin and he couldn't get them off. In his mind's eye he saw the huge, powerful jaws of the spider reaching to bury themselves in his neck. He screamed.

Later, Dwerg explained that when Alfar was initiated as an infant, there was probably some Attercop mixed in with the grease used to anoint his spine. Usually the paste was made from moles, bats, and dormice. Every now and then, though, a little Attercop would get into the goo, and that little dwarf would grow up with a deathly fear of spiders.

Now, unable to move a muscle, Alfar awaited the

fate he knew was certain to come. He saw the spider's jaws part for the bite, the poison to spew into his system. Then everything went black.

The little door in back of the closet popped open, and a bright beam from Sander's Scout light stabbed into the darkness. Sander searched over the cardboard boxes with his light and found the squirrel frozen stiff. It looked like some kind of forgotten stuffed animal left in the attic by the farmer's children a hundred years before.

Sander could see the short, rapid breathing of an animal in distress. He called softly to the squirrel. Crouching down, he stepped into the attic. The squirrel made no move as he approached, only a slight twitching of his hindquarters like a horse's withers involuntarily chasing away a fly.

Sander knew instantly what to do. He bent down as close to the squirrel as he dared, and he blew. Alfar felt the child's warm breath pass over him like a summer wind. The breeze caught the web like a sail, tore at it, and slowly, gradually, lifted it from his head. Unstuck, the gossamer mantle floated wispily upward.

Sander took another breath and blew again. Free

now, the broken web sailed off into the darkness against the rafters, and Alfar came back to himself. It was at that moment that Sander saw the small leather sack hanging from the squirrel's neck. Instinctively he reached for it, and the brush of his hand sent Alfar leaping forward across the beam and away into the eaves toward his escape.

Sander turned the sack over in his hand, regarding it under the yellow beam from his flashlight. It was empty except for a few small crumbs of honeycomb that remained in the lining. Sander couldn't help thinking that the strange bag belonged to the little man he had seen in his yard.

Back in his room, the closet door firmly shut, Sander opened the bottom drawer of his dresser and gently placed the little pouch inside next to the tinderbox. He closed the drawer carefully and quietly, afraid now that he might wake his parents and have to explain.

Outside, standing on the shingles, Alfar mused over the strange episode with the boy who lived in the farmhouse. He could feel the boy's breath blowing over him like a breeze. He shook off the memory, picked up the skep, and tapped it, emptying the bees into the hole in the rafters.

CHAPTER SIX

The old farmhouse shimmered in the midday sun. It was as if a slight vibration, like an electrical current, were running through the fiber of garden, trees, and home. Even the earth trembled ever so gently, crumbling the very tops of the summer anthills that dotted the border of the garden.

The sound, at first, seemed submerged in the crystal-clear plashing of the nearby brook. Gradually a drone could be heard, a distinct bass register all its own. It sounded like the humming of hundreds and hundreds of bees. And it was coming from the house. The buzzing was overridden momentarily by the sound of a loud, piercing shriek.

"Hurry, Sander," cried Colby. "There must be

a million of them to make this much noise. Where did they come from?"

Colby quickly spread the home section of the Sunday paper on the floor of the living room to soak up a golden, gooey mass that was dripping from the ceiling.

"Cooommmmming," yelled Sander, exaggerating the emergency to make it the most possible fun. The sound of his voice and his feet on the wooden floor increased Doppler-like with his approach.

He burst into the living room, a giant grin on his face. He waved a bright new bucket that their father had bought at the general store.

"Wow. Listen to that," Sander said, his ears perked up at the steady buzzing. "But I don't see any bees," he said, somewhat disappointed, placing the bucket under the drip.

"They must be up there somewhere in the ceiling," Colby replied. "What else could be causing *that*," she asked, jabbing her finger up at the cracked plaster overhead.

Sander froze at the bizarre sight. Colby's shriek hadn't done the scene justice. He stared at the fissure in the ceiling from which the liquid emerged almost reluctantly: a heavy spheroid tinged with gold, trembling with the vibration of the hum.

"Look. It's stained," Sander said, pointing to the long discoloration accumulating in the bucket. Without thinking, Sander stuck his finger in the bucket, scraped up a viscous gob, and brought it to his lips. He tasted the mysterious fluid with an exaggerated smacking noise.

"Oh, Sander. It might be pitch from the roof. Do you have to do that?" Colby implored.

His face lit up. So excited he could hardly speak, Sander wagged his finger and raised it for another swipe. "Honey. Colby try it . . . it's honey!"

Colby stared at him, transfixed. "Well, isn't that just perfect," she declared disgustedly. "Now we're living in a honeycomb."

Toby wandered over and poked his nose in the bucket. His long tongue lolled out and took a big lick. "See, he likes it too," Sander pointed out.

"Why don't I just leave the two of you here to enjoy your lunch then," his sister responded, stalking out.

"C'mon, Colby," Sander begged, not wanting to lose her. "Let's go upstairs and find out where this is coming from."

"Oh, all right," Colby answered reluctantly,

"but I'm only supposed to be baby-sitting you, not running all over creation."

"I don't need a baby-sitter," Sander shot back. "I'm almost twelve."

"Yeah, right. Your birthday was only a few months ago."

"What happened to you—you used to be fun," Sander lamented.

"I'm too old for fun," Colby replied.

"All right, well, baby-sit me then," cried Sander, racing out, "if you can."

His words dangled in the empty air as Colby and Toby chased after him.

Sander was up the stairs in an instant. He had a pretty good idea of where to go. He grabbed his flashlight, ran into his closet, and opened the little door leading to the attic. The humming got louder. After telling Toby to stay, he led his sister across the beams behind the wall of cardboard boxes, toward the spot where he had found the terrified squirrel the other night.

"Where are you going?" Colby asked.

"The ceiling above the parlor, silly."

Colby got cold feet. "I'm not sure this is such a good idea," she said.

"Look, it's just a bunch of bees," replied Sander.

But he didn't really believe it was that simple. The appearance of the dwarf, the squirrel with the leather sack around his neck, and now the bees. There had to be a connection. Only Sander couldn't figure it out.

"What if we get stung?" worried Colby. "You might go into shock or swell up like a balloon or stop breathing or—"

"Stop," interrupted her brother. "Somebody did this for a reason," he blurted out.

"What are you talking about?" Colby asked incredulously. "What possible reason could there be to . . ."

Her thought was never finished because, at that moment, Sander shone his light across the floor of the attic, across the lathing between the beams. Instead of wood and plaster, the slats were covered with a thick, undulating mat of bees, emanating outward from the spot where Alfar had punched a hole in the plaster.

A steady stream of bees flowed in and out of the hole, floated momentarily in the air, then flew along a draft toward an unseen passage under the eaves.

Sander was mesmerized at the sight. Colby

tugged on his shirt, whispering fiercely, "C'mon, let's get out of here. Now."

Sander allowed himself to be dragged backward slowly, behind the cover of the cardboard boxes and back into his closet. Colby shut the little door firmly, then took a deep breath.

"Oh my god, Sander, did you see that?" she exclaimed.

"C'mere," he said to his sister in a serious tone. "I think I better show you something." Sander dashed into his room and was headed for his dresser when they heard a car door slam from outside the house.

"They're back," Colby shouted from the hallway. She turned and ran for the stairs. Sander looked at his sister and resignedly pushed the half-open dresser drawer closed. Chasing after her breathlessly, he careened down the steep wooden stairs.

"Slow down," they could hear their mother yelling from somewhere downstairs. They sped, Colby leading, across the floor of the large hall that ran through the center of the main house and into the parlor that served as their living room.

They found their mother and father, hands on hips, heads bent back with eyes fixed on the leaky spot on the ceiling. The kids' arrival timed perfectly with the fall of the next plump droplet of honey. They pulled up short and noted its swift descent.

"It's honey," the children cried out, to forestall any parental blame.

Their father turned to them smiling, extending a finger sticky from his own sampling. "It's a miracle, kids," he exclaimed, not without a certain amount of pride.

Their mother frowned. "Not in *my* house," she declared.

"But sweetie, it *is* a miracle," Dad said. "Think about it—we could charge admission, pay for the renovations, put the children through college."

"Maybe we could bottle the honey and sell it too, Mom," Sander offered.

"Excellent idea, Sander," Dad said.

"After it's soaked through hundred-year-old plaster, no thank you," Colby complained.

"That's what gives it such a unique flavor," joked Dad.

"It's not funny," Mom declared, stamping her foot. "How could I possibly show the house with this mess? And it's a health hazard."

"Oh, Mom," said Sander, joining his father's side, "it's not so bad."

"The bees have to go. And that's final!" she said angrily. Then something caught her eye.

"Oh, look," she went on, disheartened. "Did you have to use that page?" She leaned down and pulled a wet sheet of newspaper off the floor. "I wanted to save that clipping on how to protect my rosebushes from Japanese beetles."

Sander watched his father shake his head.

Sander felt like a lost soul all the rest of the day. He turned down his father's offer of a game of catch, preferring to play little soldiers under the tree in the backyard, something he hadn't done since he was nine. He couldn't shake the idea that the infestation of bees was somehow his fault.

Sander tossed restlessly in bed that night. He could hear his parents' voices rising and falling from downstairs as they clashed over what to do about the bees. His father wanted to find a beekeeper and try to get the bees out alive. His mother wanted them exterminated. When he'd first seen the swarm, Sander had felt they were like a gift from the little man, but now he wasn't so sure. The bees were starting to look like trouble.

Now that it was dark, Sander was afraid of the

bees. He told himself that the parlor was at the opposite end of the house and so he had nothing to worry about. But bees were little and industrious. Who was to say they wouldn't work their way over to his end of the house and come up in the middle of the night through some crack in the old plaster walls?

Sander screwed his eyes shut tight. He was afraid of the small door in the back of the closet that led into the attic. He imagined it piled thick with bees on the other side, trying to get into his room. He had wedged his hockey stick against it to keep it shut and had pushed a chair against his closet door to be doubly sure nothing could get in. He was glad he hadn't told his sister about the little man and the leather bag. He just couldn't talk to her anymore. Especially now that they were in this strange new place. He longed to talk to Mini. Somehow, he was sure she would know what to do.

CHAPTER SEVEN

Sander ran through the kitchen past his mother, who was cleaning out the old Dutch oven. Wearing a kerchief to keep the soot out of her hair, she looked up as Sander dashed by.

"Your father's got a beekeeper coming by this afternoon to save the bees, if you're interested."

"If I'm back in time," Sander answered, grabbing his backpack.

"Where are you going?"

"Exploring with Mini. S'long, Mom." Sander slammed the screen door with a resounding bang and charged off through the barnyard.

Colby and Dad were putting the finishing touches on the old rabbit cage by the barn. Colby fed a carrot to a big fat rabbit she held in her arms while

Dad tightened a new wire door.

"Hey, Sander," she yelled to him. "Come see Sweetbriar. Isn't she a beauty?"

"Can't stop," Sander yelled back. "Man on a mission."

"What mission?" his father called after him. For a moment Sander longed to tell him.

"Top secret," he replied instead, and was off down the trail toward the brook.

Devil's Race took a long, graceful curve north. Soon the familiar fields above his home could no longer be seen through the trees on the far side of the creek. The forest thickened as Sander worked his way upstream toward an unfamiliar part of Pyngyp. He came to a sharp bend and found Mini there as she had promised. She was waiting for him next to a large dead tree that had fallen into the swirling water. Mini gave him a sunny smile. They walked in silence alongside the stream.

"I don't know about this, Sander," Mini said. "I've never been to this part of Pyngyp Woods. These old mines are sometimes flooded with water. They cave in. And even if we find the mine, what would we do if we saw this dwarf of yours?"

"We don't let him see us; then we make a plan."

"Usually you make the plan first. What makes you so sure this squirrel was the little man?"

"How else do you explain the leather sack around its neck?"

"I suppose someone could have put it there," she speculated.

"But what about the bees?" Sander insisted. "Aren't dwarfs supposed to be mischievous?"

"Or worse," warned Mini.

The banks of the stream had become so steep, it would be difficult if not impossible to climb down from the sloping shoulders. Ahead loomed another obstacle. A long, high shelf of rock stuck out from the mountain. They had run out of embankment.

Sander and Mini looked along the rocky shelf and followed it with their eyes up into the side of the mountain. It disappeared into the hillside under a spiky deadfall a hundred yards distant. They were going to have to climb up and around and hope that the embankment picked up again on the other side of the outcropping. Sander took a drink from his Scout canteen and shared it with Mini. Then he hefted his backpack, and they began their march uphill. When they reached the deadfall, they were both out of breath. Sander thought he heard an animal crashing off into the brush nearby. He looked at Mini and motioned her to halt and then brought his finger to his lips. They listened to the silence of the forest.

Sander took up a secure perch behind the deadfall and took out his telescope. He sighted toward the crest of the ridge that ran like a spine up the mountainside away from the water. He swept the spyglass over the area but could find nothing. The land dipped slightly downward and disappeared in brush before rising again into a patch of open ground along the crest.

Suddenly he saw some movement in the bushes nearby, and a deer jumped out and disappeared down into the ravine. Startled, the two children laughed. Sander shut the spyglass and put it back in its case. He turned to step out of his hiding place, and there, not five feet away, stood the Hessian. The soldier was staring directly at him, but he did not speak.

Sander was paralyzed. The soldier stood there and studied him with a calm gaze. There was no terror in his deep-blue eyes. His clothing was not yet ragged or torn, the way Sander had seen him that day on the other side of the mountain. He carried a musket in one hand and his helmet in the other.

Sander's eyes moved over his uniform, the dark-blue jacket and the crossed white belts. There was no little match tin like the one he had found, only a light rectangular impression with tiny holes where the fasteners had held it tightly to the belt. Sander instinctively felt for the tin in his pocket and remembered that he had left it at home in the dresser drawer next to the little leather sack.

"Mini," Sander whispered fiercely.

Mini gave him a blank look.

"Don't you see him?" Sander continued.

"What are you talking about?" she said.

"The Hessian," Sander stammered.

"What about him?" Mini asked.

"He's standing right next to us."

Mini looked around, then frowned.

"I don't see anything, Sander. What are you talking about? Are you crazy?"

Sander stared at her, remembering something his father had told him: that our universe is like a big crazy quilt filled with folds, and every now and then we slip into a seam and time just isn't the same anymore. It gets all jumbled up. That must be what's happening now. The Hessian is in a seam, he thought. Or else I am.

The Hessian still said nothing. He shouldered his musket and started off toward the ridge. Sander stared after him. The Hessian stopped and looked back, as if to see if Sander was following. Without hesitation Sander gathered himself and stepped out after him.

"C'mon, he's taking us somewhere."

"Sander, stop, where are you going?" Mini called to him as he started to move off at an angle to the ridge. Sander appeared to be in a trance.

The trio moved through the woods quickly and silently. The forest floor was covered with soft pine needles that cushioned Sander's footsteps, and he walked easily. He didn't feel afraid.

They crested the ridge and began a descent through clumps of tall trees toward the sound of falling water. After a while the Hessian stopped and waited for Sander to catch up with him. He stood at the edge of a clearing.

Beyond, on the far side, a series of waterfalls about fifty feet high cascaded down to feed the brook. At the foot of the falls a huge wheel, twenty feet in diameter, caught the water. The wheel turned, spilling the flood as it went. A long shaft ran from the wheel to a tall, lopped-off structure of brick and stone spewing smoke. Grimy ironworkers pushed wheelbarrows filled with chunks of ore across a timber platform leading to the top of the stone stack. They dumped the contents of the barrows down the fuming chimney, turned, and headed back the way they had come. A large bellows, driven by the waterwheel, fanned the furnace, smelting the ore. Molten iron flowed out a hole in the side of the furnace and into little furrows in the sand that looked like pigs suckling a sow. No one noticed Sander.

"Mini, do you see? Devil's Race Mine!" Sander exclaimed.

He turned to Mini, who stared openmouthed at the clearing.

"How did you know to come here?" she asked.

"The Hessian," Sander started, gesturing, but the Hessian was gone. And when the boy faced back to the gritty foundry, the scene had evaporated and the forge had disappeared. There was instead a solemn circle of stones, a reminder of ancient, crumbling walls, and a few worn timbers from the waterwheel.

"You're scaring me, Sander," Mini said slowly.

Sander took a deep breath to calm himself. "C'mon, let's find the entrance."

After a short while Sander and Mini found a tangle of wood and stone overgrown with brush where the wooden timbers framing the entrance had long ago collapsed under a pile of rocks.

"I guess that does it for the mine. There's no way in or out," Mini observed.

"Wait," Sander said, climbing up the rocks around the entrance, thinking this would make a very cool fort. He was surprised at the darkness of the shadows crowding around him.

"Looks like there's a hole there," he said, pointing to a crevice in the rockfall.

"That leads down, all right," Mini agreed. "But to where? You can't see a thing."

"Hold my hand—I'm going to look in."

"All right, but just a peek, okay?"

"Okay," Sander answered, taking her hand and leaning in as Mini braced herself against the rocks above the crevice.

"I think I see something," Sander said.

"Just hold on."

"I am. But I think it's okay."

"No, it's not. Just look."

"Okay."

"And quick, because my hand is getting tired."

Sander couldn't see the ground, and there was no handhold to help him down. If he wanted in, he was going to have to jump and hope for the best. He imagined a long fall down into a pit filled with water. The thought gave him the shivers, but he bit his lip and shut it out of his mind. He had gone too far now to turn back.

"I'm going, Mini."

"Sander, no!" Mini cried.

He let go of her hand and leaped into the darkness.

Before he hit the ground, Sander could hear the slithering and realized he had made a dreadful mistake. He landed square in the middle of a den of pit vipers. He could just make out the coppery-red heads, with the tell-tale pit between eye and nostril, and the hourglass pattern on their backs. Copperheads! His father had warned him about them. "If you can see the pit, you're too close," he had said.

He could see the pits now. The amazing thing was how many there were. He had never seen so many snakes in one place before. Milk, fox, and hognose snakes mixed with the copperheads. But there was no doubt that this den belonged to the pit vipers.

Sander sat there on the stone floor of the mine, mesmerized. Snakes were scrambling away over the rocks and between the cracks. Others were standing their ground, their tails vibrating vigorously. A big one seemed to be lining him up in its sights.

The crazy thing was that Sander thought the snakes were beautiful. His eyes quickly adjusted to the light, and he could see the dark-chestnut cross bands running wide along the sides. Thoughts of his old friends flickered through his mind. Now, *this* was a story to share at Scouts. And then the big snake struck. Sander could feel the pain of the bite, a shudder went through him, and he fell to the ground in a dead faint. The last thing he remembered was Mini's voice calling to him from far, far away.

Sander lay in a deep, deep sleep. Disjointed images of the Hessian, Indians, the little dwarf, and Mini whirled in his mind. He heard a gentle ringing of a bell and felt himself being shaken. A voice broke into his unconscious.

"Hey, are you all right?"

His eyes opened slightly, and he saw a giant shadowy figure standing over him, blotting out the sun. The shadow moved, and he was blinded by the intensity of the midday light. He moaned and tried to cover his eyes. He heard the bell jingle again.

"Here, drink some of this," the figure said, and knelt beside him.

He felt a flask of soft leather and a thick, sickly-sweet liquid poured down his throat. He swallowed, choked, and came up sputtering.

"What the heck is that stuff?"

"Goat's milk," the shadow answered, and Sander, resting on his elbows, could see for the first time that this was no giant but only a boy like himself. And then it struck him.

"Bobby?" he spoke the name softly.

"Yes," the boy answered.

"Bobby the Goat-boy?" Sander continued, shaking off the haze that clouded his brain.

"Yeah, well . . . some people call me that."

It was then that Sander noticed the kid nosing a bush by the side of the trail. The goat nibbled at the bush, and the bell jingled with her motion.

"That's Heather," Bobby said. "You must be Sander. What happened in there?"

"I got bit by a snake."

"No kidding. I saw the nest. That must be what this poultice is for," Bobby said, pointing to a spot below Sander's knee.

"What?" Sander pushed himself up to a sitting position and looked down at his leg. Sure enough, there was a sticky plaster of some kind on the side of his calf where the snake had bitten him. He felt the ache now, and he could see the wound had swollen beneath the poultice.

"Who fixed you up?" Bobby asked.

"I have no idea. How'd I get here?"

"Dunno. You were just lying here when I found you."

"Mini!" Sander sat bolt upright, the memory of the incident at the mine coming back to him in a flash. "Where's Mini?"

"She's worried sick, walking the other trail looking for you. When you didn't answer, she came and got me. We went back to the mine, but you were gone. We split up to search."

Sander took a good look at Bobby. He guessed he was about thirteen. He was a stocky boy with short dark hair and brown eyes.

"Want some more goat's milk?" Bobby said,

proffering Sander the flask again.

"Got any water?" Sander asked. He suddenly felt incredibly thirsty.

"There's a spring down the trail. It's on the way. Come on. Get up and I'll take you there."

Bobby reached down and extended his hand. Sander took it weakly, but Bobby was very strong. Sander felt himself pulled to his feet. Bobby bent and put his shoulder under Sander's armpit, half carrying him. The two boys shuffled back down the trail toward the spring.

"How's that bite feel? Does it sting?"

"Sure does. Stinks too."

"Don't worry about that. That's just horse pee."

Sander made a wry face.

"Horse pee?"

"Yup. Makes a great poultice."

About a quarter mile below Goat's Walk, Bobby headed off the trail in the general direction of the creek. Sander pulled him up short.

"Whoa. Why are we going off the trail?"

Bobby gave him a strange look.

"Because that's where the spring is."

"Have you ever noticed that weird things

sometimes happen when you go off the trail?" Sander asked tentatively.

"No weirder than the things that happen when I'm on the trail. Like finding you, for instance," Bobby replied.

Sander didn't quite know how to respond to that, so he let Bobby continue downhill to a small grotto, where a clear, cold spring bubbled out from between two boulders stacked side by side against the hillside. Sander drank deeply. He felt a little stronger. Bobby cupped his hands, filled them with water, and splashed it over his face and head.

"You've never seen anything . . . or anyone sort of unusual?" Sander went on.

"You mean like the little man?" Bobby said, very matter-of-fact. "Mini said that's who you were looking for."

Sander was floored. "You've seen him?"

"Maybe. More like I've seen signs of him. But it could be anybody. You were looking for his lair."

"At Devil's Race."

"The old mine. Well, sure, that makes sense. Dwarfs and snakes. They both like dark, stony places. And the snakes would usually keep out unwelcome visitors," Bobby said, looking pointedly

71

at Sander. "Unless, of course, the visitors don't know enough to stay away!"

"Do you know about the Hessian?"

"Mini told me, but I didn't believe her."

"I saw the Hessian today. He showed me the way to the old mine."

"So she said. Doesn't seem like he did you any favors. I guess it wasn't him who fixed you up," Bobby mused.

"Who could it have been?"

"Only one other possibility that I can think of . . ." Bobby said, letting the thought go unfinished.

"No," Sander responded in disbelief.

"Why not? He might have helped when he saw you were injured."

"Mostly he's been making trouble."

"So . . . didn't you ever get into a bit of mischief?"

"Well, sure."

"Doesn't make you a delinquent, does it?"

"Guess not. But what if you're wrong?" Sander asked wonderingly.

"Could be. Everything I know I learned from goats," Bobby said. "C'mon, let's get you back so a doctor can take a look at that bite."

The two boys rose and headed back down the hill.

Bobby's kid Heather followed, bell jingling. Mini was waiting for them at the fork. She was hopping mad.

"Promise me that you'll never do that again, Sander," she said angrily.

"Do what?" Sander asked, surprised at her vehemence.

"Leave me alone like that while you go off and get yourself killed." Mini burst into tears. The two boys stood there, not sure what to do.

"I'm sorry," Sander said sheepishly.

At the medical office, a small ranch-style house on Main Street in town, the doctor escorted Sander and his parents out of the examining room and down the hall.

"Whoever put the poultice on knew what they were doing," the doctor said. "He's going to be just fine."

"See, Mom, everything's okay," Sander said.

His mother nodded, but her expression was strained.

"We're just grateful he had a friend there who knew what to do," she said, her voice sounding thin and brittle.

Sander's sister looked up from her magazine as

they came back into the waiting room.

"You gonna live?" she asked her brother.

"Think so," Sander answered.

"Too bad," she said, grimacing.

Sander's father drove too fast on the way home. His mother sat staring through the windshield, saying nothing.

"Daddy," Colby said after he had taken a curve too quickly. "You're scaring me."

"Sorry, Colby," Dad said, lightening up on the gas pedal. "I don't want to miss the beekeeper. I'd like to get the bees out alive if we can."

"Dead or alive, I want them out," Mom said between clenched teeth, then added, "Sander, I'm worried about all the time you're spending out in these woods."

Sander could see his father eyeing him in the rearview mirror.

"But Mom, I'm exploring," he protested. "And I'm making new friends," he added.

"That's fine. You can invite your friends over to the house. We'd love to meet them."

"And you could help with the chores, you know," his sister added. "There's tons of work around the house, in case you haven't noticed. You don't ever help."

"I do too," Sander shot back. "I take out the garbage."

"Big deal. There's a whole house being fixed up, in case you haven't noticed."

"Stop the bickering, please," Mom said.

"I could use some help caning the chairs for the dining room, Sander," his father said, intervening. "It wouldn't kill you to give us a hand, at least for the next couple of days until we know that bite's all better."

Sander sank back silently in his seat. It was like hearing a prison sentence.

"Okay," he said in utter defeat.

The beekeeper's note waved from the front door as they pulled up the long driveway. Sander's father slammed the car door in irritation and went to sand the chairs on the back porch. Mom shook her head and stalked off to fix dinner.

"What's the matter with them?" Sander said, turning to his sister.

"They're fighting about the bees, and it's all your fault, Sander," his sister said. "If you hadn't gotten bitten by a snake, the bees would be gone by now.

Because of you, these stupid bees are gonna be here forever."

That night the old farmhouse resounded with the loud thrumming of the bees. The honey dripped from the living-room ceiling. A cloud of anger enveloped the Schumerhorns. Sander felt like he was indeed living in a bees' nest. He lay in bed, his leg throbbing, until he fell asleep.

CHAPTER EIGHT

The next morning Sander and his father sat out on the screened porch caning chairs. His mother and sister had picked the long, wide-bladed grasses down by the river, soaked them in the bathtub to leach out the salt, twisted them like ropes, and dried them in the sun. Now Sander and his dad wove the strands in and out across the old oaken frames of the seats. Front to back; over and under; side to side.

There was a rhythm to the work, but it was a painstaking business. Sander's reward was to apply the sleek varnish to the cane once the seat was done. He loved the dark, shiny look the varnish brought out, deep and rich.

"What else do you know about the Hessian, Dad?" Sander asked.

His father looked up briefly, his hands still working the reeds.

"Curious about him, huh?" his father asked.

"I feel connected to him in a funny kind of way," Sander said. "Because I found his matchbox."

"People make claims on us sometimes. Even after they're gone."

"You mean like ghosts."

"Not ghosts. I mean symbolically. Herder's dead. But what his life—and his death—meant is still open to interpretation."

"You're losing me, Dad. I thought you believed in spirits."

"I do. But I'm talking about the balance of good and evil in the world. If we all share the same realm yet have different powers, what keeps the balance? And whose job is it? Is it God's? Or is it yours and mine? That's the true dilemma of the spirit."

Sander looked at his father, who was smiling at him.

"How come you never give me a straight answer?" Sander asked.

"Because there are no straight answers," his father replied. "But if you want to know some facts," he continued, sensing his son's frustration, "these are the facts about your Hessian. I understand that, in the mountains, a mixed-race family, like many of the time, took Herder in. The father, a man of color named DeVries, was a former slave who escaped from the Indies and became a pirate. He later sailed under the Dutch."

"Wow," Sander interjected, "a pirate!"

"Yes," his father went on. "DeVries's success as a sailor earned him shares in the Tappan Patent, one of the early land grants, and he gave up his seafaring ways for a peaceful life and a small farm in the hills among his adopted Algonquin tribesmen."

"So why did Herder leave?" Sander asked.

"DeVries had a beautiful daughter by his Indian wife. She and Herder fell in love. Her father, however, was violently opposed to anyone who came near his daughter. When she became pregnant by Josef, her father flew into a rage. Fearing for his life, the girl urged her lover to flee. Brokenhearted, he ran."

"Until they caught up with him," Sander filled in.

"Nobody knows exactly what happened," his father finished. "But it's quite a story, isn't it?"

"Is it ever," Sander responded, wondering what his father would say if he told him that he had actually seen the Hessian.

When he had finished with the first coat of varnish, Sander looked up, and there were Bobby and Mini standing in his backyard.

"Hi," they said. "We came to see how you were doing."

Sander introduced his two friends to his father. His mom, hearing the voices, came out from the kitchen to meet them as well.

"Sander's going to be staying close to home for a couple of days," his mother warned.

"Until the bite heals," his dad added hastily, not wanting to make it seem like a punishment. "But," he continued, "we're finished here. Maybe you want to show your friends around, Sander."

Relieved, Sander quickly left the porch before his dad could change his mind, and led Bobby and Mini into the parlor with the brimming honey bucket and the buzzing of the bees. A steady drip of honey fell from the ceiling.

They looked around wide-eyed.

"Wow, listen to that," Bobby said.

"You weren't kidding, Sander," Mini added.

"You can have some honey. Much as you want," he said. Then, "C'mon, I'll show you my room."

His two friends followed Sander upstairs, where he opened his drawer and took out the little leather sack left from the night of the bees. Bobby and Mini examined it carefully.

"You tell me," Sander asked, "why would a squirrel be wearing this around his neck?"

Bobby peered inside and poked at a few crumbs.

"Looks like honeycomb," he said. "Here, Mini. Check it out."

Mini inspected the crunchy bits.

"It could've held the queen, all right," she said.

Sander stood by the window, looking out.

"And here's where I was when I saw him disappear right into thin air in my own backyard."

Mini plopped down in a chair piled with old clothes. "A dwarf in your home? Aren't you scared, Sander?"

Sander looked at her. He realized what he felt wasn't fear at all—more curiosity.

"Will you guys help me?" Sander asked.

Mini handed the sack back to Sander. "Can I see the matchbox?" she asked.

Sander placed the leather sack back in its hiding place and took out the matchbox.

"Take a look at this," he said, opening the box

and dumping the bead out in the palm of his hand. "My dad got it open, and look what was inside."

He held the bead out to Mini, who clutched it tightly.

"It must have belonged to his Indian girlfriend," Sander said. "Like a keepsake."

Mini examined the bead closely. She looked like she was going to cry. Then softly she began to sing.

> *"In the land of the tall green willow,*
> *only listen for her sigh;*
> *like night's dark curtain falling,*
> *O woman of the murmuring sky."*

Mini stopped and gave a big sigh herself. "It's the song of the soldier and the Indian girl, handed down from long ago." She picked up the tune again.

> *"Lovers fleeing the mountain's shadow,*
> *feel the Duergar curse draw near;*
> *as Pyngyp's cliffs lie taunting,*
> *a soldier's fate is sealed by fear."*

"Boy," said Bobby, "that sure was sad."

"The real story is even sadder than you think,"

said Mini, still fingering the bead. "After Herder ran away, DeVries got some of the Algonquin to chase him and kill him in the woods. But when the girl told her father how much she loved him, her father had a change of heart. He sent his youngest, fastest runners to catch up with the others and head them off, which they did. They were supposed to get Herder to come back and marry his daughter. DeVries followed after the runners as quickly as he could."

"But that isn't what happened, is it?" Sander said.

"That's right. Herder raced ahead. He must've somehow gotten off the main path to Doodletown and ended up on the cliff. Fearing the worst, he jumped. He never knew they were sent to bring him back to his love. And so he died."

"Only that isn't what I saw in the woods," Sander said, puzzled.

"What you saw is what Herder saw or *thought* he saw," Mini said. "But that's not all. DeVries strangely never caught up with his men. He never returned to the farm or was ever heard from again after that day in the forest."

"Gosh, Mini. How do you know all this?" Sander asked.

"It's the story of my family," she answered,

looking him squarely in the eye. She reached into her shirt and drew out the necklace she was wearing. Sander recognized it as the one she had worn on the day they met. She held the bead up against the necklace. It matched perfectly. "This necklace was handed down from my mother. And hers before, all the way back to the Hessian's would-be bride."

"Oh my gosh, Mini," Sander exclaimed. "You should keep it," he declared stoutly, hiding his affection for it. But she handed it back to him.

"You should hold on to it," she said simply. "Keep it with the tin. They belong together."

When they got back downstairs, an old pickup was parked in the driveway. It had once been red, but the color was now so faded, it was hard to tell where the paint ended and the rust began. Next to it stood a leathery-looking man of indeterminate age wearing filthy, dirt-encrusted work clothes. He had short, scraggly hair and the absolute blackest of hands, which were permeated with an oily stain like a tattoo. Ancient grit was caked beneath his fingernails.

The man unraveled a long hose connected to a compressor in the bed of his truck. A lit cigarette dangled from his lips. He puffed as he unfurled the hose. A grimace showed a ragged set of teeth with a large empty hole that had once held a bicuspid.

A faded yellow label on the side of a noxious-looking metal barrel declared: DANGER: LYSECTICINE. A translucent, yellowish, foul-smelling fluid oozed from under the crimped lid. An assortment of buckets, brushes, and spray cans lay higgledy-piggledy alongside the compressor.

The man grinned at the three children staring at him from the porch.

"Whaddya say, kids," he said in a tone that sent chills up their spines. "Let's kill us some bees."

Sander's mother was getting her way after all.

CHAPTER NINE

Alfar made the trek through the Highlands with great trepidation. His grandfather had summoned him to the Great Hall at Dunderburg, and he had not been home since running away. He realized now, of course, that it was useless to try to escape his grandfather. Dwerg simply had too much power. A fairy arrow with a golden shaft had been the messenger. It sank deep into the trunk of a tamarack tree along Alfar's trap line as he checked his traps for small game. The arrow howled fiercely like a summer squall down the Hudson as it arrived. The tamarack's limbs trembled, the wind itself providing Dwerg's unmistakable signature. Alfar had no choice but to obey.

From Pyngyp he followed the trail north

through the Timp Pass toward Doodletown, then turned east and up the back of Dunderburg Mountain. It was a long hike that took him the better part of the day. By late afternoon he had reached the top.

The entrance to the Great Hall was at the rear of a stone shelf at the top of the mountain and looked over the river to the southeast. Alfar made his way down into the inner recesses of Dunderburg. A winding cut through the rocks presented a near-impassable path, but within, the cave opened up and the Great Hall indeed became truly great.

The space alone was intimidating. Towering columns of stone reached from floor to ceiling. The sounds were deep and voluminous—dripping water, a stir of gravel from the movements of a small animal, a rat perhaps, and somewhere the flutter of bat wings. Alfar crossed the open floor of the cavern to a raised stone platform that stood at the base of the thickest column. There was a flat stone seat fashioned here that Dwerg used as a throne. But for the moment the throne was empty.

Alfar felt a strange, irresistible impulse to sit on the throne. He climbed up the steps and, after carefully looking around to see if he was alone, plopped himself down. He gazed around the empty chamber with an imperious glare. He felt a sudden breeze as if a door had opened somewhere, and a chill came over his bones.

"Not bad. A fair resemblance, I'd say," Dwerg's voice grated from somewhere high up in the air above him.

Alfar jumped to his feet and moved away from the throne. Dwerg's laugh resounded against the stone walls of the cavern. Alfar heard the rustle of wings, and Dwerg swooped down as a giant bat.

"Don't be afraid, Alfar. I want you to have ambition. You're going to need it."

The bat did a series of rolls, unfurling his wings to become Dwerg's black cloak and then Dwerg himself, standing on the floor facing Alfar, his arms folded. "Wasn't it ambition that brought King Goldmar to the House of von Hardenberg?" He didn't wait for an answer. "Wasn't it ambition that led him to demand a place at the table, a room in the castle, and stabling for his invisible horse?" Dwerg continued.

"Didn't he have to sing and play the harp?" Alfar asked innocently.

"It was no bargain, boy," Dwerg snapped,

annoyed at the interruption. "It was his pleasure to do so."

Alfar shrank at the rebuke. Dwerg obviously had a point to make, and Alfar was just going to have to wait until he got to it. Alfar was not much for history lessons, even the history of his own people. Or how they came to America. He tugged nervously at the brim of his hat, turning it frontward and backward.

"And wasn't it ambition that led Goldmar to destroy any who interfered?"

Alfar understood where Dwerg was heading now.

"He's just a boy. It was a little snakebite, that's all. I didn't want him cluttering up my doorstep."

"Aren't you the tidy one," Dwerg said with great sarcasm. "And I suppose, when one of von Hardenberg's servants tried to trick Goldmar into becoming visible so he could kill him, Goldmar should have thanked the man and played him a tune on his harp."

"No, Granpa," Alfar answered dully, knowing the rest of the lesson.

"No, indeed. Why, he hacked the man to death, broiled him, and ate him. Now, *there's* a lesson."

"I'm sure the servant never tried to trick old Goldmar again, that's for sure," Alfar observed.

Dwerg flared with anger at Alfar's smart remark but like quicksilver shifted to a smile.

"There you go, boy. Sarcasm. Gives you a bit of an edge. You have it in you, I know it. You want to take the throne, Alfar. And, what's more, I want you to take the throne." There was a long pause; then Dwerg added, "Eventually."

Alfar knit his brow. What was Dwerg up to now?

"Come with me," Dwerg said. "I want to show you something."

Alfar followed Dwerg back up to the mouth of the cave.

It was almost sunset. From the top of Dunderburg, the river looked like a wide, flat, glittering, silver-gray sash. It was pinched at the waist where it passed through the narrows below a smaller mountain known as Anthony's Nose on the opposite shore. It flowed royally off into the Highlands' late-afternoon sunshine, which infused the river valley with its watery light. Dwerg stood with his arm around Alfar's shoulder and waved his free hand over his dominions.

"The Shatemuc, Cahohatatia, Mohicannituck, Noordt, Mauritius, the Great River . . . the

Hudson," Dwerg intoned. "This river has been my life. And you, of course," he threw in as an afterthought. "I am the lord of everything I see, leaving off the other side where I never go. But I have a problem, Alfar. Can you guess what it is?" Dwerg smiled down at him strenuously, the corners of his mouth twisted in a grimace.

Alfar, knowing his answer would inevitably be wrong, tried valiantly nonetheless. "Bad digestion?" he offered tentatively.

"No, you idiot," Dwerg spit out, in spite of his attempts at restraint. "I have no family," he said, with an attempt at infinite sorrow.

"But you've got me, Granpa," Alfar replied.

Dwerg snorted, then contained himself. "I do. Yes, yes. I do have you, Alfar, for which I am eternally grateful."

"Why, thank you, Granpa," Alfar said, feeling complimented.

"Don't thank me yet," Dwerg said curtly, then continued. "What I meant was that I don't have descendants . . . I mean, after you, what is there?"

"No one," Alfar agreed. "I guess I'm the end of the line."

"That's just it, Alfar," Dwerg responded. "You are

the end of my line." He paused, letting the thought sink in more deeply, then added, "Unless we do something about it."

Alfar was thinking very hard now. He waited for the other shoe to drop. "Yes, Grandfather," he said hesitantly.

"Fortunately, I do have a solution. In fact, it's quite brilliant if I do say so myself. It is the ultimate lesson in becoming a full-fledged Black Dwarf. It also gives you the perfect revenge for your father's murder. And it will ultimately provide me with the heir to carry on my name and lineage. You will of course name the baby after me."

This last remark threw Alfar completely.

"What are you saying, Granpa?"

"You must take a fairy bride. You will steal a human child—in this case, a girl descended from those who killed your father. You will marry her. And when she is of age, she will bear your son, my great-grandson, and the next great Lord of the Dunderburg."

"But who?" Alfar questioned, fearing the answer.

"That girl. That friend of your little snakebit boy. What's her name?"

"Minisceongo."

"She's the one," Dwerg said with finality.

"What about her friend?" Alfar asked worriedly.

"Don't worry. He's just a pest. You worry about the girl . . . and my great-grandson."

In a grand gesture he swept his arm across the horizon. "Just think, my boy, one day all this will be . . . his."

Alfar stared at his grandfather in distress that Dwerg mistook as selfishness.

"After you're through with it, of course," he added hastily.

Alfar watched Dwerg out of the corner of his eye and wished his father were there to tell him what to do.

Alfar sat by a fire in the open ground beyond the mouth of Devil's Race Mine. For the first time in a long while he sought the space and air of the outdoors. The fire was laid on a few remaining chunks of granite that had been part of the foundation of the old furnace. He ate from a tin of dried beef that he had stolen from some hikers on the other side of the mountain. The beef tasted salty and good. As he ate, Alfar thumbed through a book of spells until he came to a chapter heading on fairy brides. He chewed the beef and read by the light of his small campfire.

Later, with the fire's embers banked, Alfar lay on his bed of soft pine sprays, freshly plucked from the lower limbs of the trees near his cave. He could see the vast expanse of night sky above him. Though his dwarf soul usually yearned for dark, enclosed spaces, tonight he was filled with a sense of wonder. The moon was hidden and the black sky was shot through with stars.

Dwerg had told him that the universe was a grand machine. Like the intricate workings of a gigantic celestial clock, it spun in space and slowly ticked away the centuries, unwinding into the dark vastness of a space too big to imagine.

Not far away, Sander and his father were squinting up at that same canopy of stars.

"I feel bad about the bees," Sander said as they lined up on Albireo, a pretty double star at the foot of the Northern Cross.

"I feel like the shepherd Aristaeus, who was punished by having all his bees killed, and then he had to go to the abode of the gods and wrestle with Proteus to learn what sacrifices to make to get them back."

"I don't think those bees are coming back," Sander said gloomily. "And the only person you had to wrestle with was Mom."

"Disappointed?"

"I guess," Sander said.

"The Historical Society is coming, and the bee-keeper was away on a fishing trip. We really couldn't wait," his father said.

"You mean Mom couldn't wait," said Sander. Then he changed the subject. "Did Aristaeus get a constellation?" he asked.

"Nope. There's the Beehive cluster in Cancer, but you can't see it until winter. And it doesn't have anything to do with Aristaeus, I'm afraid." His father looked at him. "Had enough?"

"I'm tired, I guess," Sander allowed. "I don't think I can stay up for the meteor showers tonight. Do you mind?"

"Let's pack it in, then. I'm ready for bed too," his father said. "One thing about the universe. It unwinds exceeding slowly. That means when you miss something, you often get a second chance."

Alfar stared toward the horizon and the invisible Canopus lurking below that luminous star of the southern sky, the primordial egg from which all things were born. Tonight marked the new moon, and with it would come the Perseids, with their flaming arcs, to torch the night with their brilliance. Alfar breathed in his loneliness like the piney air. It rarely troubled him, but tonight he felt it. Alfar tried to picture his mother's face in the sky, but it wouldn't come. Overhead, in the great vastness of the night sky, fiery streaks of light rent the inky blue-blackness above him. The Perseids had come in full glory.

CHAPTER TEN

The guests from the Historical Society were, for the most part, men and women in their sixties who appeared, to Sander at least, to be old enough to have been close personal friends of the original occupants. They moved through the house like visitors to a museum. They paused reverentially before each detail of antique and architecture, slightly canted forward in a listening pose, as if the objects were about to disclose some whispered secret from the past.

A long wooden table was set in the barnyard off the door to the summer kitchen. The table, its red-and-white-checked oilcloth snapping in the breeze, was set with dishes of fried pickled pork and sugared apples, succotash, and apple cider.

Sander's father was engrossed in a conversation with a short, round, bearded fellow with glasses and a shock of dyed black hair that seemed to stand straight up from his head. Sander's mom set down a platter of olykoeks fried in lard, made from Mini's recipe, as Sander ran past. "Where's your sister?" she called after him, but he paid no attention. She shook her head, looked around for her daughter, and frowned.

Then she smiled at one of the visiting women surveying the table. "Help yourself," she said brightly. Other guests began to crowd toward the table, eager to sample the classic Colonial country cuisine.

Dwerg shook Alfar awake. "For Goldmar's sake, boy," he exclaimed with a fury. "Do you enjoy flouting the laws of the Duergar? Napping in the open like this. What if this were dawn instead of noon? You'd turn to stone, and then where would I be? Can't you remember anything I've taught you? 'First light, eternal dark.' Weren't you listening? Must you always mock the old ways?" Dwerg complained.

Alfar rolled over and sat up blinking into the sunlight. "Oh my" was all he could manage.

"Get up, you lazybones. I want to show you how we get rid of a pest."

Dwerg swept up his cloak, the wight furling furiously around him.

"Watch and learn, my little pudding dreams," the wight warned.

The cloak fell to the ground. An animal shape moved around under it, turning this way and that as if looking for a way out, like a small dog. A shiny black nose appeared, lips curled, teeth showing, followed by a long face, fierce bright eyes, and a coat of red fur. A fox. The fox jumped out suddenly and stood facing Alfar, grinning, as if ready to pounce.

"It takes a clever fox to catch a hound," Dwerg growled. "And I plan a merry chase. Just you wait and see. Now come, follow me, and see how it's done."

The fox gave a yelp and was gone in a flash, racing across the clearing into the woods running down along Devil's Race toward the old farmhouse. Alfar struggled to his feet, rubbed his eyes, and trudged after him. Realizing he could never keep up, Alfar changed his mind and cut across Devil's Race a quarter mile downstream from the old foundry. The route would take him through

Blackwater Marsh on the other side, but then he would be in the meadows that ran north of the farmhouse and could make up the lost time.

Sander ran alongside the barn to the empty rabbit cage, its door wide open. A miserable Colby searched for Sweetbriar in the brush behind their father's compost pile.

"Darn you, Sander," his sister said.

"I told you I didn't do it," Sander answered, a whine creeping into his voice. "I never messed with your darn rabbit."

"Somebody opened the cage. Who let her out? Sweetbriar, Sweetbriar," Colby cooed.

"Rabbits don't come when they're called," Sander said in disgust. "She's not a dog."

"What are we going to do?" Colby asked plaintively.

"Let's get a nice big bunch of lettuce and carrots, and maybe she'll come back when she gets hungry."

"Okay," Colby said halfheartedly.

They had barely made it back to the kitchen to hunt for vegetables when her mother stopped Colby, summoning her to kitchen duty.

"But we're looking for Sweetbriar. She's lost."

"She's probably gone back to the wild, where she belongs. And anyway, now is just not the time."

"What if she's close? This may be our only chance to find her," Colby insisted, refusing to give up.

"Then I'm sure she'll be back before you know it. Now take these trays out to the table. We're all out of pork, and our guests are going hungry."

"Sander," Colby whispered fiercely as she exited. "It's up to you."

The screen door banged closed behind her. Sander blinked. He wasn't sure what to do next. He watched his mother bend over the stove to retrieve the next batch of olykoeks, her back turned. He saw his opportunity.

Sander had hardly opened the refrigerator door, intending to sneak some lettuce out, before a great cry rose up from the party of guests gathered around the table outside. Toby added his warbling howl to the general din. Sander saw his mother's head shoot up. She stood frozen to the spot by the oven like a witch in a fairy tale, holding the pan of olykoeks.

The screen door flew open. It was his father in a high pitch of excitement.

"Sander," he yelled. "Get the BB gun."

Sweetbriar had turned up just as Sander's mom had promised, though not remotely as she had imagined. The rabbit was tearing in great loopy circles around the backyard, pursued by a scruffy red fox.

The fox chased Sweetbriar. Colby chased the fox, screaming for him to stop. She waved a fistful of fried pork to get his attention off the rabbit. Toby had taken up the chase as well, and the mad procession of rabbit, fox, girl, and dog wound in and out among the trees and around the lawn furniture, knocking chairs and tables flying as it went. The guests gaped and Sander's father joined in the chase, last in line.

"Oh goody, a reenactment," a florid-faced old woman observed with delight, bending toward a wizened old gentleman next to her. "Yes, must be. I think it's that story about the runaway johnny cake."

Sander knew instantly that this fox-who-would-not-be-shooed was no ordinary fox. Why the little man was pursuing Sweetbriar he had no idea, but he made his mind up to stop him. His first shot with the BB gun went wide of the mark and struck the round, bearded man on the right buttock. Sander saw the guest jump, his hand reaching back instinctively to stop the pain. Sander would have smiled if events had not taken such a serious turn. He swung the rifle over the runaway train of animals and people and tried to set his sights on the fox.

Mom snapped out of her shock and burst from the kitchen. She stood frozen on the threshold, aghast at the scene in front of her, holding the screen door ajar. Sweetbriar, sensing an escape to freedom, made a run straight for the open door. Between the rabbit and safety, however, was the length of the picnic table with its heaping serving platters. Undaunted, the rabbit took a great flying leap and dashed across the top, scattering apples, succotash, and olykoeks as she went. Dwerg, a few steps behind the rabbit, leaped after her, jaws wide. Whatever Sweetbriar missed the fox bowled over with unerring swiftness.

A cacophony of shattering crockery rose up over the farmyard. A shower of cider splashed from the bowl, its ladle catapulted skyward as the whirlwind tore down the picnic table. The fox had gained on the rabbit and was now only a foot behind. His muscles bunched for a leap, and Sander knew the next shot had to count.

He fired and hit the fox in the flank, forcing a painful cry. The fox lost his balance in midair and fell, crashing heavily to the ground. Sweetbriar shot off the end of the table right into Mom's arms. The fox rolled to his feet and ran off yelping, with Sander on his tail. Colby ran up to her mother, who cradled the quaking rabbit like she was a baby. Mom's mouth hung open, speechless.

Colby took Sweetbriar back to her cage beside the barn. The guests stared and, one by one, put down their plates carefully among the shards of pottery and indistinguishable clumps of food on the soaked tablecloth. They quietly slipped around the side of the house to their waiting cars. The secretary of the society took Mom by the elbow, gave her a sympathetic smile and nod, and without a word left after the others.

Mom was close to tears. Dad came up to his wife and put his arms around her to comfort her. She closed her eyes and pressed her face into his chest. Toby waggled up and curled at their feet, panting hard from his exertions. Sander was nowhere to be seen.

The fox limped along through the meadow above the barns. "Ow, ow, ow," he said. The fox sat down and attempted to lick his sore flank. He craned his neck around but wasn't used to the body he was in.

The sore spot remained just out of reach. "Shoot me, will he? The little dickens. I'll show him." He rolled to his feet and sniffed the air. "And where's my useless grandson? Now he's going to miss everything." Dwerg snorted in disgust and loped off awkwardly down the hill through the tall grass toward the water.

Sander, his BB gun slung across his back, tracked the fox through the meadow. It wasn't difficult, since Dwerg, despite his injury, had made a point of trampling the grasses to leave an obvious trail. The farther he got from his home, the less sure Sander was of what he would do when he caught up with the little man.

The trail led to a low stone wall. Sander climbed over, assuming the fox had jumped, wounded or not. He found himself in an unfamiliar meadow.

Across the creek was the rocky shelf that had blocked his path the day the Hessian led him to the old mine. Yet this side of Devil's Race was different. There was a backwater here off the main branch of the creek. The pasture sunk down to the water, and the tree line led to a forbidding swamp, Blackwater Marsh.

Sander picked up the fox's trail. It led straight down toward the swamp. He followed and stood at the edge of the marsh, trying to decide what to do next. At that moment he caught sight of the fox, dragging his rear leg across the clay muck and disappearing into a thick clump of marsh grasses. Sander plunged in after him.

A dozen yards ahead the fox paused. His ears pricked up, and he listened to make sure the boy was following. A sucking sound, as Sander's foot pulled free of the quickening earth, satisfied him. He chuckled to himself and headed deeper into the swamp. The lame leg drew a wiggly line in the soft, damp, sandy earth behind him.

Sander found the going tougher now as patches of water forced him to circle about, seeking a path over more solid ground. The water was indeed black, Sander noticed. Each time he thought he had lost the fox, he would catch a glimpse of quick animal movement somewhere ahead, dimly seen through the grassy clumps that thrust up from the scabrous surface of the swamp. The chase would resume.

The grasses were now as tall as he was, and he could no longer see the forest or the meadow as reference points. His feet sank deeper and deeper into the mud. He realized that he was no longer leaving a trail and could not retrace his steps. He was lost.

Still, he wasn't ready to give up. The air was filled with the sounds of clamoring insects, bird cries, and the distant sound of running water from Devil's Race. He was sure the fox was close.

Only a few feet away, hidden by a rotten log, Dwerg paused to catch his breath and observe the little hunter. He could tell now that the boy was totally lost. "By Goldmar," Dwerg exclaimed to himself, "my work is done. The swamp can claim him."

The osprey rose suddenly, startling Sander. It must have been right next to him. He spotted the hulk of log half buried in the mud. The great bird stretched its enormous, mottled, gray-brown wings and let out a piercing cry. It flew right at Sander, snapping its beak as if to strike. Sander ducked instinctively, and the bird rose up, circling, as if to mock him, then rose higher and higher into the sky and sailed off away from the quagmire of Blackwater Marsh. Everything was still. Sander felt completely alone. He knew too, although he could not fathom the connection, that the fox was gone as well.

A short distance away Alfar also heard the osprey's cry and watched the great bird rise above the swamp. He had chanced the shortcut through the swamp, but it was clearly a mistake. The sun was high, he had no sense of direction, and he had lost his way. He had been wandering for over an hour.

He looked around him again. The brownish mud was flat and looked packed and stiff on top but quaked slightly with each step. It was as if the muck were a thick skin stretched over some foul black liquid. The sun had begun to tip, and he detected a slight change in the way the light shone on the blades of marsh grass as silver turned to gold. Judging the sun to the west, he shivered and struck out toward the south. He hadn't gone more than a dozen yards before he heard something moving through the swamp, headed in his direction.

Alfar froze in fear. He stifled the impulse to flee. He couldn't hope to outrun any animal in the mire. He kicked himself for leaving the belt of invisibility in his cave. If only he had practiced, as his grandfather had told him. But it was all too late.

In his panic Alfar didn't watch his footing. He landed in the soup. Quicksand. He could feel the wet, grainy morass sucking at his ankles. He tried to loosen his legs. But he was stuck and sinking fast.

Quickly sinking up to his jerkin, Alfar stared

wildly around him, caught in a mystery he could not comprehend. He stopped struggling. He knew it only made things worse and would bring him to a quicker end.

He could feel his weight pulling him down. Mouth open, he struggled to breathe, the sand pressed against his chest. Fear of suffocation constricted his breathing even further. He shook his head at the thought of this ultimate disappointment to his grandfather. His final failure. He realized at that moment that Dwerg would never know what had happened. Alfar would simply disappear, and his grandfather would think him a coward who ran away.

Absurdly, he took off his cap and tried to sail it to the near edge of the marsh so that it would mark his passing. The cap fell short and lay on top of the quicksand several feet from the sure ground. The next rain would probably sink it, too.

He stared dumbly at the rust-colored baseball cap, his dilapidated memorial. The grasses beyond the cap parted, and Sander stepped out onto the edge of the quicksand, facing him. Sander gasped at the sight of the little man half buried in the sand. He started to walk forward.

"Watch out!" Alfar cried out instinctively,

forgetting that he was making his enemy safe to sit and gloat at his distress. Sander stared open-mouthed, clenching his BB gun. His anticipated confrontation with the little man was not turning out as he imagined.

"What should I do?" he asked earnestly.

"Leave me alone," Alfar said disconsolately. "Just leave me alone to die."

Sander quickly searched the rim of the quicksand with his eye, confirming he was already at the short-est possible distance to Alfar—about six feet away.

"Don't move," he ordered.

"Please," Alfar protested weakly, knowing how cruel little boys can be. He craned his neck sideways and tried anxiously to follow Sander.

Sander dropped his rifle and circled the patch, looking for something. He found an old rotting tree branch and pulled it free from the muck. It was about three feet long and two inches thick. He ran back to face Alfar and raised the branch over his head with both hands, judging the distance. Alfar flinched and raised his arms to keep from being hit in the face. Sander tossed the branch. It landed and broke into several pieces in front of Alfar.

"Aaaahhhhhh," exclaimed Alfar, frightened,

helpless to stop the barrage he was sure to come.

"Darn," Sander said, glowering at the useless pieces of wood.

"Just go, please" Alfar begged plaintively. "Isn't this enough?"

Sander stood at the edge of the quicksand. His hands were on his hips and he was thinking very hard. He sat down on the wet ground and pulled off his muddy sneakers. He pulled his shirt over his head and took off his pants.

Alfar watched in amazement as the boy, standing in his underwear, quickly fashioned a rope of his clothes. He tied one end of his shirt to his BB gun and the other to a pant leg. Perhaps the boy was trying to help him after all. But it was too little, too late, Alfar thought.

Sander had made a crude life preserver, and he stretched it out on the shore, trying to gauge the length. It was short and he knew it. He was going to have to wade in a couple of feet from the edge. Without hesitation, Sander picked up the rig and stepped into the quicksand toward Alfar.

"No. What are you doing?" Alfar cried.

Sander felt himself sinking but, holding his breath, he took another step, bringing him even closer. He was almost up to Alfar's baseball cap.

"Steady," he said, as much to himself as to Alfar.

Sander halted, his breath coming in short, shallow gasps. He could feel the sand grabbing him now, sucking him down. He couldn't delay another instant.

Alfar could see him sinking. "Get out," he said fearfully.

"Grab onto this," Sander ordered, and tossed the rifle out in front of him while clutching the pant leg. The rifle plopped onto the quicksand just at Alfar's outermost reach. His stubby little fingers stretched and latched onto the trigger guard, dragging the rifle toward him until he clenched barrel and stock in a firm grip.

"Hang on," Sander said, and began to pull. He was down to his knees in the quicksand. He yanked on the pant leg with all his might, but nothing happened. He guessed the little man was about his weight, but without a firm footing he could do nothing. He looked Alfar in the eye. The little man was staring at him with a look of hope.

Sander smiled at him and said, "Let's try it again." At that moment Sander's feet touched bottom, the hardpan that lay beneath the quicksand and trapped the watery muck. He was in the shallows.

He wriggled his toes to make sure and then threw himself into his task with renewed energy.

"All right." His voice was stronger now. "Pull."

Alfar hung on to the rifle, and this time the quicksand gave way. He could feel himself being squeezed up and out. They repeated the process several times, each effort loosening the marsh's grip on Alfar until he lay almost prone on the surface, within arm's length of Sander. A long gouge in the muck marked his progress toward the shore.

"Okay, drop the rifle and give me your hand," Sander said, his own fully extended.

Alfar did as he was told. He reached as far as he could, stretching his arms until first their fingers, then their hands, clasped. The rifle and clothes lay where they had fallen, muddied and wet. Sander gave one final heave and Alfar came free. The two tumbled backward onto solid ground. They lay on their backs, panting. Sander laughed.

"Wow, that was really scary," he said.

Alfar propped himself up on his elbow and looked straight at Sander. "You saved me. Why?" he asked.

Sander sat up and looked back at him, shaking his head. "Chasing a rabbit isn't a capital offense. Unless maybe you ate her."

"What?" Alfar stared at him quizzically, not understanding.

"Why did you crash my mother's party?" asked Sander, answering his question with another.

"Oh," Alfar replied, starting to realize what had happened. "That wasn't me."

Now it was Sander's turn to be confused. "Who was the fox, then, if it wasn't you?"

"I'm afraid you must've had a little run-in with my grandfather," Alfar said.

"Your grandfather?" Sander said skeptically.

"Dwerg, the Lord of the Dunderburg," Alfar explained helpfully.

"Well, I shot the old geezer in the butt with my BB gun."

"That would only make him mad," Alfar observed ruefully.

"I chased him here," Sander continued. "He was limping pretty bad."

"He would want you to think that," Alfar said.

"You mean it was a trap?" Sander's eyebrows knit together, and he could feel a tingle go down his spine.

"What happened to me was meant for you," Alfar explained. "I was supposed to meet him, but I was late, so I took the shortcut and ended up where you found me. He was leading you straight to it."

"Who are you?" Sander asked.

"Alfar, son of Rahbad, grandson of Dwerg, a Black Dwarf and a twenty-fifth-generation descendant of the great Duergar king Goldmar." He gave a stiff little bow of his head.

"The great king who?" Sander asked in disbelief. "Never mind."

"Mini told me about Dwerg. I thought he was a legend."

"Oh, he's a legend all right," Alfar said. He took his head in his hands and shook it back and forth woefully. "This is a terrible thing grandfather's done."

"Mistaking murder for mischief is pretty serious," Sander agreed.

Alfar looked Sander in the eye once again. "It gets worse," he said.

"But we're okay," Sander insisted. "Just muddy, that's all. My mother would kill me except I think she's too upset right now."

Alfar ignored this last remark and looked up at the sky. The sun was clearly moving over to the west. "Okay," he said, getting to his feet. "I think I can find our way out now. Come with me. When we get to the creek, you can wash your clothes."

Alfar stood up and Sander followed his example. They collected Sander's things, and carefully skirting the patch of quicksand that had nearly claimed Alfar's life, the pair slipped away into the marsh grasses, heading back the way Alfar had come.

At the big turn in Devil's Race, the water foamed against the rocks on the near side. The backwater collected in a natural pool before overflowing into the low-lying marsh. Sander's clothes lay on the rocks, drying in the sun as he lolled in the water kicking his feet. Alfar sat on the stone watching him. His baseball cap shaded his eyes from the afternoon sun. Horseflies buzzed above the surface, nearly skimming the water. Sander brought one down with a big swat.

"Got him. Why don't you come in, Alfar?" he asked.

"Dwarfs don't like water," Alfar answered. "Unless it's dripping from the ceiling or collecting on the floor."

"Ugh," Sander said. "That sounds nasty." He pulled himself up and out of the water and sat on the hot rock, dangling his feet next to Alfar.

"I guess I should be getting back now. My folks

will be worrying about what happened to me," Sander said.

"That sounds nice," Alfar said, "having someone worrying about you."

"You don't have anyone to worry about you?" Sander asked, curious. "Where are your parents?"

"They've been dead for a long time."

"Sorry," Sander said, and meant it. He couldn't imagine a world without his parents. "What about your grandfather?"

"Oh, Dwerg worries about me all the time, but not like that. He's just worried about how much damage I'm doing to his legend."

"He's mean. Someone should tell him that people aren't talking about him anymore anyway," Sander said helpfully.

"They will be soon if I do what he wants me to do," Alfar said.

"What's that?" Sander asked.

Alfar chewed on his lower lip and thought about whether to share his terrible secret.

"He expects me to kidnap Mini and make her my fairy bride. We would live in the fairy world forever, and Dwerg would eventually have a great-grandson to carry on his name and tradition."

Sander's eyes were wide. "Oh my gosh, Alfar. You can't let that happen," he exclaimed, horrified. "Mini's just a girl."

"A girl descended from the Indians who killed my father. So Dwerg says," the dwarf continued. "He says revenge is the true path to becoming a Black Dwarf. If only I had made serious mischief years ago, he might've been satisfied that I was powerful enough to continue his line. Now it's too late."

"You have to refuse him," Sander insisted.

"How? You see what comes of tangling with Dwerg," Alfar said. "He always gets what he wants."

"Not always," Sander said thoughtfully. "I'm still here, aren't I?"

"You lead a charmed life," Alfar replied.

"Well, what if I were to help you? Me and Bobby and Mini could beat him."

"But what can children do against black magic?" Alfar asked, worried about Dwerg's inevitable retribution.

"I don't know," Sander said bravely. "But we've got to try." Sander quickly put on his still-damp clothes. "C'mon, I want you to tell me everything about Dwerg and the Black Dwarfs. We've got to go warn Mini."

Alfar led Sander back upstream, and together they crossed the brook just below Devil's Race Mine. They leaped from rock to rock, and Sander marveled at the little man's strength, speed, and sure-footedness. Sander was out of breath by the time they reached the far shore. Alfar turned to see how Sander was keeping up. His face crinkled into a semblance of a smile. He tugged on his baseball cap, crooked his finger, and gestured for Sander to follow. He disappeared into the underbrush that grew along the creek. Sander pressed through the scrub brush and found Alfar waiting for him on the trail.

They made a strange pair, the boy and the dwarf, as they walked quickly through the forest. Alfar slackened his pace to favor Sander and told him the story of his family as they went.

"Alfar, have you ever seen the ghost of Hessian Falls?" Sander asked. Alfar turned and gave Sander a penetrating look.

"You never know what you're going to run into when you go off the trail," he said.

"Then you have," Sander pressed him.

Alfar nodded. "He's a poor soul. But he's harmless."

"I thought so too, until the snakes," Sander replied.

"He couldn't have known about the snakes," Alfar said.

"Thank you for fixing the bite," Sander added politely.

Alfar gave a little bow.

"The Hessian's cursed. He can't leave this place. He's condemned to wander these woods and repeat his last hours," the dwarf answered.

"How do you know?" the boy asked.

"Dwerg," the dwarf answered simply. "DeVries's men lost the trail, so Dwerg conjured Mohawks to follow the Hessian through the woods and chase him to the top. Until the only way out was down. He said it was revenge for my father, but I think he does things like that for his amusement."

"What did the Hessian ever do to anybody?" the boy wondered aloud.

"His only crime was to love," Alfar said sadly.

Sander shook his head in disbelief. He was beginning to see the dimensions of Dwerg's cruelty and power.

Sander stared Alfar straight in the eye. "Your grandfather's right, you know. You're not cut out to be a Black Dwarf."

"I know," the dwarf answered, his head sinking down.

"Don't be ashamed," Sander said to cheer him up.

"You're more like a White Dwarf, if there is such a thing," the boy continued. "You know, like a good fairy." Sander's eyes sparkled.

"I'm afraid my powers for good are no stronger than my powers for evil," the little man answered.

"Maybe we don't that know yet," Sander observed.

Alfar agreed to meet the rest of the little group later, and the two parted company at the fork in the trail below Goat's Walk. Alfar headed back down the mountain. Sander shouldered his BB gun and continued alone to the old shed the kids had picked as a meeting place. He made his way through the rubble of Goat's Walk. He heard the bright tinkling tones of a single bell and realized that the young goat, Heather, must be somewhere close at hand. He found her nibbling in a grove of jack pine just off the trail. She followed him to the shed. He had forgotten all about the fox, the wreckage of the Historical Society luncheon, and his mother's broken dreams. All he could think about was how to save Mini.

CHAPTER ELEVEN

Mini and Bobby the Goat-boy listened with rapt attention as Sander described his adventure in the swamp. The three were holed up on the lower slopes of Goat's Walk in the ramshackle timber hutch used by the tenders of the old icehouse. It was full of cobwebs and birds' nests. A hornet sailed in and out of the broken windows, circling the tumbledown shed. A section of the roof had fallen in, and lazy summer clouds could be seen floating in the pale-blue sky overhead. Devil's Race roared below them.

"Climbing a mountain. Defeating the Lord of the Dunderburg? This is crazy, Sander," Bobby the Goat-boy said, folding his arms and sitting back against the wall of the little cabin. "What does this little dwarf need us along for?"

"Alfar can't face his grandpa by himself. We're his courage," Sander replied.

"But isn't Mini the one Dwerg wants?" Bobby said. "We'd be serving her up on a silver platter. It's too dangerous for her to go."

"He needs a bridegroom as well as a bride to have his revenge. Mini's no use to him unless Alfar cooperates," Sander countered.

"Sander's right, Bobby," Mini interjected. She had been sitting quietly for some time, trying to absorb all she'd heard. "If Alfar can't stand up to his grandfather, I don't have a chance."

"But Mini," Bobby protested. Mini held up her hand and cut him short. "Thanks, Bobby, really. But this is about what happens to me. And there's always the hope that . . ." She broke off and looked suddenly teary.

"What is it, Mini?" Sander asked, lowering his voice.

She snuffled and pulled up her chin into a defiant pose. "That the revenge just has to stop. It's against the laws of nature."

"Somebody should tell Dwerg that," the stocky goatherd said.

"I will." Mini glared fiercely. "If I have to."

"Bobby, are you with us?" Sander asked gently.

Bobby nodded. "Of course. If Mini gets trapped in the fairy world, who would help me look after the goats?" His face split into a wide grin. His crew-cut hair stood up straight on his head. Mini smiled sweetly at him.

"All right," Sander said decisively, rubbing his palms together. "Here's my plan."

The sun was long gone over Pyngyp, and the mountain's shadow darkened the hillside by the time Sander reached the foot of the trail at the log crossing near home. He could hear his father's voice calling, echoed by his sister's.

"Dad," he yelled back. "I'm here."

He met them at the creek and, on the walk to the house, told them of his unsuccessful attempts to hunt down the fox. He left out the part about Alfar in the quicksand and Dwerg's plot against Mini. Nor did he breathe a word about what he was about to do.

They walked around through the barnyard to the back of the house. The table was cleared and the broken plates cleaned up. His mother, who had been up in her room for most of the afternoon, crying by the look of redness in her eyes, met Sander at the kitchen door. Relieved to see him in one piece, she let her worry flare up as anger.

"How could you run off like that, Sander, especially after that business with the snake? I've been worried sick about you all afternoon," she said.

"Mom was about to call the police when you showed up, Sander," Colby added.

Sander put his head down and shrugged his shoulders. "I'm sorry," he said.

"Put away your BB gun and go wash up. Tonight we're having macaroni and salad, okay? No old Dutch food. Not for a while, anyway."

Sander and his sister exchanged relieved looks. Mom heaved a sigh and headed for the kitchen to fix supper.

Dinner at the Schumerhorns' that night was a dispirited affair. Sander looked around the table at his family as they ate. His sister was closemouthed. His mother was too unhappy to put a good face on things. His father chewed his food deliberately and said nothing. Sander broke the silence.

"The house looked nice today, Mom," he said.

"Yeah, Mom, it did," Colby added.

"Thank you both," Mom said. "You all worked very hard, and I want you to know how much I appreciate your help." She looked at each of them and added softly, "And I know I pushed you all. Maybe too much." She looked straight at Sander's father. He caught her eye and smiled, nodding.

"It's not fair if they blame you for what some stupid animal did," Sander said.

"They won't, Sander, don't worry," his mother said. "It was just so embarrassing."

There was a pause for a moment; then a smile crept up on Sander's sister's lips.

"You should've seen the look on your face when Sweetbriar jumped into your arms," she said.

"I guess I looked pretty ridiculous," Mom said.

"You sure did," Sander added. "And those Historical Society people were all standing there with their mouths hanging open. I bet they had never seen anything like that in their entire lives."

"And didn't you shoot Mr. Conklyn in the butt with your BB gun?" his father said.

"No!" Sander's mom exclaimed, horrified.

Sander looked sheepish. "I think so. He kinda jumped like he was bit by a horsefly."

They all laughed.

"But promise me you won't run off again like that, Sander, please," his mother said. "Stay close to home, won't you?"

Sander froze. All he could think of was his plan to meet Mini and Bobby later that night. He didn't want to lie, but he didn't know what to say. So he said nothing.

"I'm sure you can find something to do around the house, can't you, Sander?" his father asked.

Sander smiled his hollow smile but still didn't know what to say.

"Something wrong, Sander?" his father asked.

"Something you want to tell us?" his mother added, growing suspicious.

"Sander," his sister said plaintively, "why don't you answer them? What's the matter with you?"

"Excuse me" was all Sander could manage. He pushed his chair back and ran from the table, upstairs to his room.

After dinner Sander came quietly back downstairs and went outside. He stood in the front yard. He could feel the dark shape of Pyngyp rising off in the darkness. Overhead he could just make out the constellation Aquila, the eagle. With wings outspread, it seemed to soar through the sky. Its brightest star, Altair, glowed yellowish-white against the black-velvet drapery of night.

Sander thought about the intricate past of this strange place that was now his home. History, the kind his father studied and taught, was really only a pale shadow of life. For all Sander could tell, so much more existed than ever made its way into books. He felt very small in this knowledge. He heard the door open behind him and his father's footsteps on the porch.

"Seen any meteors yet?" he asked.

"Saw a big one a minute ago. It whooshed all across the northeast," Sander replied.

"I remember when I first got curious about the stars, I used to sneak out of the house after I was supposed to be in bed, just to look at them."

"Did you get caught?" Sander asked.

"Eventually. I stayed out too late and fell asleep in a chair on the porch in my pajamas."

"Did Grandpa and Grandma get mad at you?"

"They checked on me every night for a week to make sure I was asleep. Then they forgot about it."

"Were you a curious kid, Dad?" Sander asked.

"Sure, aren't all kids? Whoa, did you see that?"

his dad said, pointing up to the faint path of a shooting star tracing across the sky.

"A beauty," Sander said. "So—what if you're on the trail of something important that you just *have* to do but that the rest of the world might think is a little crazy?"

"I can tell you what my father said. 'Better to beg forgiveness than to ask permission.'"

"You're always quoting people. What do *you* think?"

"I can't tell you what to do, but I'll give you one piece of advice, which you can use anytime you're in a jam."

"What is it?"

"If you can remember this, you'll always be okay." He paused for effect. "All you've got to do is breathe."

Sander's eyebrows went up.

"That's it?" Sander said, disappointed.

"That's it. Just breathe."

Sander lay on his bed, trying to rest until his parents went to sleep and the house was quiet. Then he took his old backpack out of the closet. He checked its contents: rope, knife, flashlight and batteries, olykoeks and pork that had been saved from the fox's rampage on the picnic table, and a canteen full of water. Satisfied, he zipped it closed. He had decided not to take the BB gun because of the extra weight and its limited usefulness against the powers of Dwerg. On impulse he opened his dresser drawer and took out the tin matchbox. The bead rattled. He put it in his pocket. It was almost midnight.

Sander waited a full hour. The house was dark and silent when he got up out of bed. He crept downstairs and out the front door without disturbing Toby. In a few minutes he stood at the edge of Devil's Race. There was a three-quarter moon in an almost cloudless sky. The moon gave him plenty of light, even in the forest, at least until he reached the deep pines. Sander knew the trail pretty well, but everything looked different at night.

He met Alfar as planned on the other side of the stream, and the two trudged up the hill toward Goat's Walk, where they were to meet Bobby and Mini. Although the walk was maybe a mile as the crow flies, on the trail and in the dark it still took a good while to reach the stony rockfall.

Sander spotted Bobby's chunky silhouette standing out against the lighter gray of the rocky slope at the end of the trail before it led to Goat's Walk. It detached itself from the shadows on the forest floor and met Sander in a pale pool of moonlight.

"I can't find Heather," Bobby cried, waving his arms anxiously. "She's lost."

"We can't worry about her now, Bobby. She'll be okay."

"But I *am* worried. I haven't heard her bell ring all night."

"She'll turn up, believe me," Sander repeated, trying to calm him. "We have bigger fish to fry. Where's Mini?"

"I dunno. She should've been here by now."

"She has to come up the trail. Let's cross and go on until we meet her," Sander said impatiently.

The trio set out across Goat's Walk. Alfar's sight was keenest, especially in the dark, but they followed Bobby, who knew the way better. Together they crossed the stone slope to the forest on the other side and down the trail along Pyngyp's flank to Mini's house. Bobby slowed the group when they reached the gorge. Here the footing was more treacherous, and Bobby warned his companions to be careful. Sander slipped first. He bumped his knee heavily in the dark, fearful of sliding over the edge of the precipice that they all knew lay below. Alfar grabbed his arm and helped him to his feet. They all took a collective breath, and the little band pushed on.

Sander guessed that it was about two thirty A.M. when they finally scrambled down the last few hundred yards of the trail. Something was wrong. They should have met Mini by now. Sander was afraid that she might have somehow strayed off the trail in the dark. If she had, she might even now be lost in the strange world out of time that he had entered twice since his arrival. He hurried anxiously past Bobby.

The last leg of the path to Mini's house picked up at the foot of the main trail and ran for a couple of hundred yards along a small stream. The path passed by the family cemetery where Mini's great-great-great-great-grandmother was buried, crossed a small stone bridge over the stream, and ran right up to Mini's back door.

Sander expected the house to be dark, but lights seemed to be on in every room, upstairs and down. He could see the headlamps of a car in the driveway on the far side of the house and hear the rumble of its engine. Sander, instantly worried, turned to Alfar and Bobby and told them to go back and wait for him by the witch-hazel trees while he went to find out what was going on. The dwarf and the Goat-boy turned back and hid in the grove while Sander tiptoed around the side of the house.

He could hear the rising and falling of voices from the living room. He crept alongside the house and peeked through the window. He saw Mini's father, distraught, talking with a grim-looking police chief. It was not hard to make out the words. Mini was missing. Kidnapped, her father feared, or worse. She had never made it home after their meeting in the shed above the icehouse earlier that afternoon.

Sander gasped. This changed everything. He was too late. Dwerg had decided not to wait for Alfar and had stolen Mini himself. He kicked himself for leaving Mini alone for those few precious hours. He never should have let her out of his sight.

Sander turned back and raced to the grove to find his friends. There was no time to lose now. They hadn't even set out on their journey, and Dwerg already had the advantage.

The trio moved quietly through the dark, retracing their steps to the base of the mountain. The loss of Mini weighed heavily on the little group. What had started out as a voyage with glorious prospects had now taken on a cast of desperation. Alfar, who was leading the way, raised his hand to bring the boys to a halt. He turned to face Sander.

"Is your mind still made up, boy?" the grizzled dwarf asked pointedly of Sander, his voice grating with nervousness.

"More than ever," Sander answered with determination.

"Because once we leave, there's no going back until it's done," the dwarf continued ominously. "The Highlands are a different world, and travelers aren't welcome."

"I'm not afraid of the Lord of the Dunderburg," Bobby chimed in bravely.

Alfar turned, squinting to see the boy's round face in the moonlight.

"Well, I am, boy. I am," Alfar said with finality.

His words hung briefly on the night air. Sander broke the silence.

"That's why you're with us, Alfar. Now let's get going," he said impatiently. He started up the trail back over Pyngyp. Alfar stopped him abruptly.

"Not that way. We can't go overland. Dwerg has spies all through the woods." The dwarf turned and headed down the little stream.

"Where are we going?" Sander asked.

"To the river."

Alfar's slightly bowlegged form swayed as he moved along the stream in the moonlight. He stopped and beckoned to the two boys, who stood frozen at the last moment. "Are you with me?" he asked, silhouetted against the gently flowing water.

"We're coming!" Sander and Bobby the Goatboy snapped out of their momentary funk and hurried to catch up with Alfar.

The flatland along the stream grew wider, and their progress became easier when they found a solid dirt path. As they walked, the stream grew broader and faster.

"The roads are gone now. You're in the Highlands—just as they were two hundred years ago," the dwarf said.

Sander could hear Bobby's sharp intake of breath at the news. There really *was* no turning back. Sander squared his shoulders and pushed on after the dwarf.

Cloud scud covered the moon and thickened until there was no more light. Sander's flashlight shone brightly for a while, then gave out. He rapped it several times against the palm of his hand. It blinked weakly, then was gone. He was glad he had packed the extra batteries, but he fumbled trying to find them in the dark. Even Alfar, who never seemed to need a break, could see that the boys were too tired to go on. He suggested that they rest for a while until the sun came up and then continue on their way. They tried to make themselves comfortable, but the boys were so exhausted that they simply nestled down in the soft damp grass by the edge of the stream.

Before he dropped off, Sander could make out Alfar's shape standing still in the darkness a few yards away. He was erect, alert, and peering toward the woods. He had picked up a stick along the way and held it like a cudgel. Sander realized he was keeping watch.

A breeze brought a rich, ripe smell. He sniffed the air and tasted the faint scent of salt on the back of his throat. There was a rustling sound of tall grasses and small watery splashes of animals slipping into the shallows. Underneath all the sounds was the constant rise and fall of the cicadas, scraping their hind legs like a thousand tiny violinists in a mad summer concert. He realized they had reached the river. And then he fell sound asleep.

CHAPTER TWELVE

Alfar woke Sander and Bobby two hours later. The sun had not quite broken the horizon, but the morning light revealed a watery expanse of tall rushes, pussy willows, and cattails. Beyond lay the broad, flat plain of the river. Sander listened to the sharp cries of gulls wheeling overhead.

Bobby the Goat-boy blinked and yawned. "Where are we?" he asked, sniffing the cool morning air.

"The Prince Mauritius River. Otherwise known as the Hudson. And Kumachenack Bay," Alfar said. "All my birthright, in fact, according to my grandfather."

"Isn't this Grassy Point?" said Sander. He remembered coming here, where the river was at its widest, with his sister and parents soon after their arrival to look for rushes to cane the chairs. They had driven across the Penny Bridge on the bluff above the marshy floodplain that connected the town to the point. But the Grassy Point he remembered was gone. There was no road, no Penny Bridge, just the bluff rising above the wetlands.

Alfar pointed to the foot of the bluff, his arm describing the route they would take through to the bay on the other side and then continuing north along the river to the Dunderburg. But the boys complained that they had to eat before they could go any farther. Alfar shrugged his shoulders. He was not so familiar with the habits of people in general and children in particular. He sat back down.

Sander offered his companions a quick bite of olykoeks and pork before they renewed their journey. Each ate his small portion with relish, and they took turns sipping water from Sander's canteen.

The sun came up brilliantly as they ate, and their spirits rose. The river beyond the marsh gleamed with the dawn, and their hearts filled with hopefulness.

"Alfar, what do you think Dwerg will do when you tell him you won't cooperate?" Sander asked as he passed his canteen to the dwarf.

"He might turn me into a toad," Alfar said, wincing.

"But couldn't you just turn yourself back again? After all, you turned yourself into a squirrel that night in my attic."

Alfar nodded his head slowly. "His magic is too strong. I can do squirrels, mice, sparrows. Little animals of no consequence. Nothing big or scary like Dwerg. He can do owls with sharp eyes and sharper claws. Wolves with great dripping fangs. Mountain lions." Alfar was scaring himself with his catalog of Dwerg's transformations. "Once he attacked some campers as a black bear. Tipped their trailer right over."

"Wow," Bobby said, raising his eyebrows, duly impressed.

"Don't you practice?" Sander asked. "I mean, I could hardly tie my shoes when I joined the Cub Scouts, but I wanted to get a merit badge in knots. I had to practice every knot in the book every day until I had it down."

"You sound like my grandfather," Alfar said with a wry grin.

"But maybe he has a point, Alfar," Bobby added, seeing the possibilities. "I mean, this job could go a lot easier if we had a couple of tricks up our sleeve. . . ."

"Yeah," said Sander, filling with enthusiasm. "Show us what you got, Alfar. C'mon."

The little man took off his baseball cap and scratched his head.

"I dunno," he said. "It's not the kind of thing you do in public. Even Dwerg uses a cloak." Alfar's face was turning red with embarrassment.

"Cloak, schmoak," Sander replied. "Try something bigger than a squirrel."

"Yeah," Bobby added excitedly. "Even a dog would be good. But a big dog, like a schnauzer."

"It'll help build your confidence," Sander added persuasively.

"Oh, all right," agreed Alfar. He took off his hat and reached into his back pocket and pulled out his Bible, handing them to Sander. "Here, hold these."

Sander felt the greasy, sweat-stained hat, and a surprised look came over his face at the sight of the old Bible. The look registered on Alfar.

"I like the Old Testament," he acknowledged sheepishly. At the last minute he took the hat back. "Better hold on to my hat. It's my good-luck charm," he explained, putting it back on.

"So," the boys said in unison, "let's see you do it."

Alfar's eyes closed and his head drooped. His

long arms hung at his sides. The air seemed suddenly very still. A hush had fallen over the riverbank. Even the gulls seemed to stop their screeching. For a long moment nothing happened, and Sander felt a sudden giddy flush of foolishness. Then Alfar began to tremble. His eyes rolled back in his head and his whole body began to quake.

Sander and Bobby the Goat-boy looked at each other, frightened. It dawned on them that they might have started something with terrible consequences. Alfar flipped over and landed on all fours. He twisted his face up into a ferocious grimace, lunged at Sander, and began yapping like a dog. Bobby laughed at the silliness of it.

"Look, Sander, he thinks he's a dog."

The transformation was instantaneous.

Alfar's yapping turned suddenly into a deep-throated growl. And where the little man had knelt, rear end wagging, there now stood an enormous black hound with flaming orange-yellow eyes. Only the red baseball cap perched on the dog's great head signified that Alfar was somewhere within. The muscles of the black hound's chest and shoulders were bunched as if to spring. His mouth was opened wide, and he had huge, gnashing teeth, dripping with blood-flecked foam. The hound snarled at Bobby, who shrieked in terror.

"Whoa," said Sander under his breath. Now, this was really something. "Alfar," Sander continued soothingly. "Easy, boy, easy." The black hound slowly turned his huge, fierce head, burning eyes, and slavering mouth toward Sander. He took a step forward and the boy shrunk back against the riverbank. He realized that he and Bobby were trapped. If the hound decided to strike, there was no hope for them.

"Come back, Alfar," Bobby intoned gently. "Good boy, Alfar. You did a good job. You can come home now."

The hound growled once more, took another menacing step forward, then pulled up short with a yelp as if he had been hit. His rear end tucked under, and he began running in circles as if to avoid a spanking. Sander and Bobby stared wide-eyed. The hound's body began to tremble, as Alfar's had a moment before. A huge bulge seemed to explode from inside the hound, and his side heaved as if something inside were struggling to get out. The thing imploded, and his body was suddenly as thin as a greyhound. Then it exploded again like a giant balloon. This time the bulge from inside pushed far out, and Sander and Bobby could see a perfect impression of Alfar's face on the side of the hound. Then the dog imploded again and the face was lost.

The circling hound began to make a sputtering sound, and he stood up balancing on his hind legs. With the baseball cap he looked like a performing dog in a circus. And then the hound transformed again. Only instead of turning back to Alfar, he became a series of crazy compound animals. A bear's head growled on the body of a snake standing on the haunches of a goat. A lion's face roared on the body of a horse with the great scaly tail of a crocodile. A giant frog flapped the broad wings of a heron on the skulking hind end of a skunk.

Alfar had become like a child's toy whose heads, bodies, and rear ends are switched to create a bizarre bestiary. Sander and Bobby gasped. This was more terrible than they had imagined. What if Alfar couldn't get out? He would be gone, and they would be marooned forever—*if* this strange con-glomeration of animals didn't eat them for supper. The amazing thing was that Alfar's baseball cap stayed on the entire time.

The transformation stopped as abruptly as it had

started. The winged-frog–skunk thing tried to take off. It lifted a few feet off the ground, then crashed in a heap of animal parts. The air was filled with the cries, yowls, and calls of innumerable beasts. The parts shuffled themselves in a frenzy, then collapsed in an indistinguishable mass, which reassembled itself into Alfar. He was lying on his back, arms flung out, panting hard.

"Water," the little dwarf croaked.

Sander leaped to his side with the canteen, followed closely by Bobby, who held the dwarf's head. Alfar lapped up the water greedily like a thirsty dog. His chest heaved up and down.

"That needs a little work," he managed to get out finally.

"Alfar," Sander said, impressed, "you were magnificent."

"Yeah," Bobby agreed. "I don't know about Dwerg, but you sure scared the living daylights out of me."

Alfar sat up, and they helped the little man to his feet. He handed Sander the canteen and dusted himself off with his hat. "Thank you, Bobby. Sander. Like you said, practice." He looked up at the sun. Dawn had given way to morning light now as the sun was up in full. He looked at the hummocks of grass standing above the waterline.

"Low tide. Better shove off," the dwarf said, and the boys collected their things. Alfar picked up his cudgel and gestured toward the lowlands at the foot of the bluff. "This way," he said. "We'll cut across the point to the bay."

After about a half hour's march they reached the smaller bay on the other side of the point. A more prominent bluff stuck out into the narrowing river at the bay's northernmost end opposite them. A long, curving swath of tall marsh grasses lined the shore leading to the bluff. They descended into the grasses and moved along the shoreline.

"You sure this is the easiest way?" Bobby complained to Alfar.

"I didn't say this was the easiest. In fact, it's the hardest. It's just the most secret," the dwarf replied.

"I'll say it's secret. I can't see a thing," Sander added, pushing his way through the tall stalks, his feet sinking into the soft, sandy bottom.

"Just follow me. Once we cross the next headland, we'll have more solid ground and can start making some time," Alfar said.

They emerged from the grasses and crossed a short, sandy stretch of beach until they reached the foot of the bluff. It was covered with an impassable jumble of thick, thorny underbrush. The little band pulled up short. Alfar stood, tugging at his chin. It was humid and buggy here, and Sander and Bobby quickly began swatting at hordes of mosquitoes that seemed to fly right into their eyes and up their nose.

"Snfffff," snorted Bobby, blowing a bug out of his nostril. "Buggy."

"Now what, Alfar?" Sander asked.

Alfar didn't get to answer.

"These'll do," a gruff voice broke in. "Let's take 'em."

There was a shout, and a dozen ragged-looking men ran out of the ravine from a hiding place in the brush. Sander couldn't believe his eyes. They were a gaggle of swarthy, muscular men with squinty eyes and rough, tanned, leathery skin and bare feet. Judging by their seamen's clothes, the cutlasses they gripped, and their fierce looks, they could be only one thing.

"Pirates," Bobby the Goat-boy said with a whistle.

"Pirates," echoed Alfar.

"Pirates?" wondered Sander aloud.

"Pirates is right, laddie," the leader of the group, a bosun's mate, growled.

The pirates all seemed to be missing parts: hands, legs, eyes, fingers, and toes and teeth by the score. Among them it seemed as if they might have a full complement for only two or three of their number. As they limped slowly toward them, Sander wasn't sure whether he should run away or stay and help them.

The leader brandished his sword menacingly. The bosun's mate was a one-eyed jack. He stumped along on a wooden leg. A few of his fingers were missing. He came over to Sander and looked him up and down.

"These boys'll make fine seamen. At least after the cap'n gets through with them," he said, leering.

"Look," one of his compatriots called out behind him, "they're all in one piece!"

"Twice't as good," muttered another. "Do the work of two men."

"And looky here," the leader said, turning his attention to Alfar. "This one's a dwarf."

"Now, that'll please the cap'n all right," a short, stout sailor who was missing three fingers on one hand and two on another said, grimacing. "He has a particular dislike for dwarfs."

Alfar shuddered.

Sander looked down the beach and spotted their longboat where it lay concealed in the marsh grasses. A trap. And they had walked right into it.

The three were herded toward the longboat and splashed dutifully out into the shallows at sword-point. The pirates fought over Sander's bag, dumping the contents out on the beach before the bosun's mate could stop them. They marveled at the flashlight and batteries. They poked them with a stick and jumped back as if they were some kind of explosive charge. The bosun's mate snatched the bag away from them.

"Leave off there. The cap'n'll want to be havin' a look at this." He scooped up the flashlight and batteries from the sand. "'Ere now, climb aboard," he said roughly, shoving Sander and Bobby the Goat-boy up against the gunwales of the gently rocking longboat. "You can forget about whatever business you were on," he said as they hoisted themselves in. "You're with the press gang now. And soon you'll be manning the bilge pumps of the finest ship to sail the Mauritius."

There was no room on the seats for the prisoners, so they sat uncomfortably in the few inches of muddy river water at the bottom of the longboat. The pirates all climbed in after them. The bosun's mate took the tiller, and each man took an oar. Those with missing arms sat together, the right with the left, to make a sure two-handed grip. At the mate's signal, the pirates shoved off and began the stroke in unison. Their course would just skirt the rocky shelf. Noting the captives' downcast gaze, one of the sailors took pity on them. "But cheer up, lads, a life at sea is not so bad. Look at us." Sander raised his head. The boatful of mangled sailors grinned back.

When they reached the tip of the headland, Sander could see a long stretch of the river open up to the north. There, just off shore, lay the pirates' ship, a small-masted, fore-and-aft-rigged sloop, a vessel built for speed and maneuverability to prey on coastal shipping. It rocked gently at anchor, gun ports closed, and looked for all the world like a peaceful craft readying itself for a pleasant day's sail up the river.

The longboat pulled alongside and made fast. Sander could see upon closer inspection that the ship was a lot like the men who sailed her: a patch-work of jury-rigged repair, holes crudely covered with boards; the sail a crazy quilt of shreds of cloth sewn together. A knotted rope ladder that looked like it had been spliced a hundred times came clattering down from above. Sander, Alfar, and Bobby the Goat-boy scrambled upward to the deck. The seamen took somewhat longer, helping one another to overcome their various infirmities.

The three travelers hit the deck and were greeted by a strange sight. A slight breeze whistled in the rigging. An idle flap of canvas stirred lightly. A wave slapped against the side. Otherwise, the ship was ghostly still. There wasn't a single sign of life. They stared around them in disbelief.

The bosun's mate was first up behind them. He landed on the deck and shrugged. "You see we're a bit short of men, able or otherwise." He sniffed the air and looked around. "'S quiet now, but we've a fearful voyage ahead." He gestured to the empty quarterdeck. "Cap'n's below. He'll be wanting to see you," he said, jabbing one of his remaining fingers at Sander and Bobby. Then, turning to Alfar, he added for punctuation, "And especially you."

The mate led the boys and the dwarf

belowdecks. The low ceilings and narrow walkways felt confining. Sander calculated that they were heading toward the stern of the ship. They arrived in a line, with Alfar bringing up the rear, at a thick wooden door that led to the captain's quarters. The door was closed. The mate scrutinized his charges, knit his brows in a worried expression, afraid that they—and by implication he—would be found wanting, then knocked with trepidation.

A muffled voice answered. The mate couldn't make out the response and so leaned close and put his ear to the door. "It's bosun's mate Cathcart, sir. With the 'volunteers' you asks for, sir. Reportin' for duty." The muffled voice spoke again, but the mate still couldn't make it out.

"Eh, Cap'n?" He pressed harder against the door.

The door wrenched open suddenly as the captain stepped into the gangway, and the mate fell to one knee, gripping the door frame for support. A deep voice boomed, "I said come in, Cathcart, come in."

The three "volunteers" stepped back as one, bumping into one another as they did so. The captain was a tall, powerfully built man of color. His brown skin was like fine-grained leather, lined and wrinkled from the years at sea. His features were a striking combination of Native American, African, and perhaps Portuguese or Dutch. He was an imposing figure.

"Cap'n DeVries," the mate said by way of introduction, getting to his feet and recovering his duty, "the new men, as you requested, sir." Sander froze, recalling Mini's story of her pirate ancestor of the Ramapoughs so long ago. DeVries, holder of the Tappan Patent. Of course, thought Sander, these would be his waters. But DeVries had retired. He lived off the land. It didn't make any sense. What was he doing here? Sander didn't have time to think.

Cathcart's eyes lit up with the sudden recollection, "And oh, sir, you may be pleased to note," he went on, "that one hiding in back's a dwarf, sir."

A dark expression came over DeVries's face as the mate rattled on. "He knows it won't go well with him, sir, that's why he's hanging back."

With a single angry sweep of his powerful right arm, DeVries brushed the mate and the two boys to one side and stood glaring at the cowering Alfar in the corridor. Alfar's head was down.

"You," DeVries said in a commanding tone. The sound of his voice was chilling. Sander felt himself pressed hard against the wall by the captain's strong right arm, and he realized there was nothing he could do to help Alfar.

Slowly Alfar raised his head. DeVries's penetrating eyes searched Alfar's face, then abruptly his expression changed with a flood of recognition. "You," he said again, only this time he softened, the harshness left his voice, and he seemed to be struggling. "But you're dead," the pirate said, uncomprehending. "I saw you die."

Now it was Alfar's turn to be confused. He looked at DeVries quizzically. Cathcart looked back and forth from his captain to the dwarf, utterly at a loss to understand what was going on. DeVries collected himself instantly. "The three of you. In my cabin. Immediately," he said with great authority. Sander, Bobby, and Alfar jumped to do his bidding. They scooted past the dumbly curious bosun's mate, who stood openmouthed before his commander, and entered the captain's cabin.

"Dismissed, Mr. Cathcart," DeVries said summarily. Cathcart was a beat too slow. "I said dismissed," the captain snapped, "or I'll take the cat to you myself."

Cathcart came to life at the threat of a flogging.

"Aye, aye, sir," he said, and hightailed it for the safety of the upper deck.

"And pass the word for Mr. Bissell," the captain called after him. Mr. Bissell was his first lieutenant and had stayed aboard during the press-gang expedition.

The captain's cabin was a simple, spare room with a wooden trestle table and a few chairs set before a long window that looked out from the stern across the river. A sleeping hammock was gathered on a hook on one wall out of the way to make more room in the daytime. Next to the hammock was a wooden chest and a smaller wooden table that held a basin. A small glass mirror hung on the wall above it for shaving. DeVries had to bend his head to duck the cross timbers as he made his way to the desk and sat down. His desk was littered with charts. A sextant and a brass telescope rested on his papers. His sword was slung in its belt across the back of his chair. He studied Alfar, Sander, and Bobby the Goat-boy standing before him.

DeVries picked up the sextant and held it before him. "Navigation," he said, "is an art. When you know how to plot your position by the stars, you can sail anywhere in the world. It's a tremendous freedom." He threw the sextant against the wall, and the boys jumped at the impact.

"But I don't need a sextant to plot where I'm going. You know why?" Each of the captives shook his head slowly, fearful in the face of the captain's mercurial flashes of anger.

"Because I know exactly where I'm going." His eyes bored into them. "You know why?" Again his captives shook their heads slowly from side to side.

"Because I've been there before." He glared again. A knock came at the door. "Come in, Mr. Bissell." The door opened, and Mr. Bissell appeared. He was a broad-shouldered man with a mustache. He didn't seem to be missing anything, Sander noticed.

"Wind's up, Cap'n," Mr. Bissell said, "and—"

"I know, I know," DeVries interrupted wearily. "The tide's coming in."

"Yes sir, Cap'n," Mr. Bissell acknowledged.

"Well, up anchor and make sail, Mr. Bissell."

"Our course, sir?" Bissell asked.

"Horse Rack, Mr. Bissell. Do you have need to ask?" DeVries answered.

"No, sir. Aye, aye, sir," Bissell said. He turned on his heel and left the cabin. Now Sander could see that, despite the long hair that had overgrown the spot, his right ear was missing. The door closed behind the lieutenant, and DeVries turned his attention back to the dwarf and the two boys.

"We've sailed through Horse Rack every day for the past two hundred years, and yet he persists in asking. As if we might go somewhere else," he finished bitterly. "You see, many years ago I made a foolish bargain. I was in Antwerp preparing to set sail for the New World, and one night there came a knock at my door. It was a dwarf. Taller than you, I might add," DeVries said pointedly to Alfar. "He proposed a passage for his family, in return for which I was to enjoy the greatest of worldly success. I was no longer to be a pirate, an outcast, but a respectable man, landed even, with the grant of the Tappan Patent. And all I had to do was to take this old kobold's family along on my journey. It made no sense to refuse."

"Dwerg," Alfar said. The word escaped his lips.

"Exactly," the captain said regretfully. "Dwerg," he repeated, almost to himself.

"That's Alfar's grandfather," Sander jumped in, unable to stop himself.

"Don't interrupt," DeVries barked, and Sander became instantly still. They could hear Bissell shouting orders above decks and the laboring of the cable hawser as the anchor was raised.

"Alfar, is it?" the captain asked, looking straight at the dwarf. "Then the little man I saw drown must have been your father."

Alfar started like a bolt of lightning running through a tree. "Rahbad," he whispered.

"Amazing resemblance," DeVries went on, ignoring Alfar's stunned response.

"They were hiding in the stores for the crossing," he said. "I couldn't let the crew see them, superstitious as they are. So I made Dwerg swear never to come out on deck. We hit a storm in the North Atlantic, and the ship was tossing about. It was so bad, I had all the men below except for a skeleton crew. I was at the helm, and I saw your father climb out of the hatch and try to make his way to me. He was gesturing wildly, but the wind blew away his words. Then a huge sea crashed over the ship. I was roped to the helm, but when the water ran out of the scuppers, your father was gone."

"Why, why . . ." Alfar, astonished by DeVries's version of events, stumbled, unable to get out the words.

"Why was he on deck? Your mother was in labor with you, and Rahbad decided she needed a sawbones. He was coming to me to ask. Dwerg wouldn't come. And then, of course, he blamed me for his son's death. Your mother made it through after all."

Sander, Bobby, and Alfar had listened in amazement. DeVries paused for a moment in reflection. They could feel the ship get underway, hear the sound of the wind filling the canvas, the groaning of the beams, the alternating slap and thunk of feet and wooden legs on the deck as the crew hurried to their jobs.

"But how did you come to be here?" Sander asked.

"Dwerg likes to savor his revenge. He bided his time. Years later he sprung his trap when I was alone in the forest. He kept me from saving the one person who would ensure my daughter's happiness, the Hessian soldier. And he doomed me to an infinity of servitude on this ship, sailing the treacherous narrows of Horse Rack in endless fairy punishment."

It was Bobby the Goat-boy who broke the silence. "But sir, that's why we've come. . . . We're on our way to the Dunderburg to destroy Dwerg."

Alfar and Sander looked at Bobby. DeVries turned to Alfar. "Go up against your grandfather? Your own blood?"

Alfar stood as tall as he could. "My father's blood runs in my veins. And my mother's, and they were both good dwarfs," he said firmly. "This time Dwerg must be stopped."

"He has your great-great-great-great-grand-daughter, sir. Mini, sir," Sander rushed in. "He's kidnapped her and plans to imprison her forever just like you . . . sir," he added as an afterthought.

DeVries quaked with visible anger. The others drew back instinctively. "My granddaughter," he managed to get out in quiet fury.

"Great-great-great-great—" Bobby added, but DeVries cut him off. He stood up sharply, his chair scraping against the floor.

"Enough," he said, and drew his sword from the scabbard. It gleamed sharply in the watery light that filled the cabin. Then DeVries halted. "Do you hear it?" he asked.

The three allies leaned forward together, listening. All they could hear was the sound of the ship moving through the waves as it started to run upriver with the incoming tide. "What, sir?" Sander asked.

"Why, the wind, lad," the captain answered. "Dwerg's wind. She comes. He sends her down the mountain to destroy us. You've seen my men. They're being whittled to pieces by Dwerg's infernal wind."

They could hear the gathering storm now. DeVries ran to the chest and opened it. He withdrew a small bow and a quiver of arrows. He handed them to Sander, who lashed the gift to his backpack. "Take these. I stole them from Dwerg himself. You'll need them to fight his fairy spirits."

He turned to Alfar and took him by the shoulders, the huge pirate towering over the little dwarf. "What a shame. I could have used the crew. But Dwerg must be stopped. And my great-great-great-great-granddaughter must be freed."

He took a short sword from the chest and handed it to Alfar, who stuck it in his belt. Sander noticed Silverstorm for the first time. It was of beautiful hammered silver, the shiny scales circling the little man's waist. DeVries rummaged around for a moment longer, looking for a talisman for Bobby, but couldn't find one. He turned to Bobby empty-handed, but Bobby was holding his slingshot in his hand.

"I'm already armed," the Goat-boy said.

"Good man," DeVries said. "Quickly now, men. To the deck. Follow me." DeVries grabbed his brass telescope and hurried out of the room, with Mini's would-be rescuers following close behind.

The weather had changed drastically in the short time that they had been belowdecks. The wind was whipping the surface of the river into a substantial chop. The sails were bellied out and straining at the mast. "Are you mad, Mr. Bissell? Reef those tops'l gallants."

Mr. Bissell, at mid decks, heard his captain calling and tried to reply that they needed the extra sail to make up for the later start, but the captain waved him off. He turned back to the men aloft. They were a terrible sight, hanging on for dear life while trying to take in the canvas.

Sander realized how far upriver they had come. The point could no longer be seen behind them. The gray-green wall of Mt. Anthony's Nose lay to starboard. And off to the port side, dimly seen behind a rapidly approaching squall, rose the grim granite facade of the Dunderburg.

"I'm going to put in as close as I can to Kidd's Humbug," DeVries said to Sander.

"Kidd's Humbug?" Sander asked.

"Aye, Cap'n Kidd. The old rascal was supposed to have buried treasure there, but I know better.

Money slipped through his fingers. The man couldn't hold on to a two-handled jug. He was flat broke when he died."

DeVries shook his head. "Take the longboat," he said, "and make for shore just there by Satan's Toes." He pointed with his finger toward a series of smooth rock outcroppings that projected into the river. The water crashed over the rocks. He handed Sander the brass telescope. Looking through it, Sander could just make out Kidd's Humbug, a small, protected cove lying at the foot of the Dunderburg just north of Satan's Toes.

"You'll have to lower the boat yourself," DeVries yelled, raising his voice against the shrieking of the wind and gesturing to the longboat rocking in its stays. "Every able man is aloft." There was a scream and a crash as one of the pirates fell to the deck, his fall broken by a cask of water. The cask splintered, and the water splashed upward in a fountain. The man raised himself up, grinned at the captain, and waved his hook to signal he was all right. In a flash he was on his feet and back up in the rigging.

DeVries turned and yelled to his first lieutenant, who was at the helm, "Mr. Bissell, I'll have you make two points to starboard, if you please."

Bissell gave him a look as if his captain had gone mad. "You heard me, Lieutenant. And now."

Bissell followed his direction, and the ship veered off from the main channel toward Satan's Toes. The sloop steered straight for the squall. The storm raced over them with a vengeance. The rain came down now in torrential sheets. You could barely make out the land from mid river. Sander, Bobby, and Alfar raced to the longboat and began to lower her down the side of the ship. The sloop was pitching in the wind, and the longboat swung out and away, then came crashing back against the side with a horrendous crunching sound.

DeVries, realizing the gravity of the situation, grabbed the lines to steady the longboat while the three climbed over the railing of the sloop, ready to jump. Sander leaned out to gauge the distance to the boat. He felt wobbly. They were going to have to time their leap carefully when the longboat next bashed against the ship. Sander looked down at the foaming gray water beneath him and the closing gap as the longboat swung back. The longboat crashed into the side once again and Sander could hear DeVries yelling behind him, "Jump, lads, jump for your lives!"

The three rescuers all leaped together. Alfar, Sander, and Bobby the Goat-boy landed in a heap at the bottom of the longboat. They could feel DeVries lowering them as they struggled to their feet. They were almost to the water by the time they regained their footing. Sander made ready to cast off the line while Alfar took the tiller. Bobby grabbed an oar and took his seat.

The way the river was heaving, they were going to have to fend off quickly or risk being run over by the sloop as she came about. She was going to have to tack fast back toward the main channel, or she would run aground. As it was, she was at the breaking point, undermanned and strained by the fierce wind and tide. She might heel over and sink like a stone. Or drift onto Satan's Toes and be pounded to pieces.

Sander cast off the moment the longboat touched the water. He grabbed an oar with his free hand, and together he and Bobby used the oars to push off against the heavy timber of the sloop. As soon as they were clear, they leaped to the thwarts and began to pull for their lives. Sander could see DeVries looking after them over the railing. He barked an order, and the sloop began to move away as her helm came over. Sander lost her in the driving rain, but he had no time to think about what would become of DeVries and his crew. They were in enough trouble of their own.

The two boys were no match at the oars for a dozen practiced seamen. The longboat was tossed this way and that by the wind and the waves. It appeared they might capsize at any moment. Gradually they made a little headway, and Sander could see the waves breaking over the rocks. He tried to yell to Alfar to steer above the rocks, but the gale made it impossible to be heard. He jabbed his finger, and Alfar nodded his head. He turned the tiller to take them above the rocks, but the boat wouldn't respond. Sander and Bobby threw their backs into their rowing once more and tried to turn the boat with the oars, but it was no use.

The longboat was heading straight for Satan's Toes. The river ran high and fast, squeezed by the narrows and the tide. Water boiled around the gray rocks. The wind had reached gale force and the chop was wild, whipped into a sea of foaming peaks. They were caught in the grip of a powerful current, and it was taking them right onto the rocks.

"What should we do?" Bobby yelled in Sander's ear, leaning over as far in his seat as he dared.

"We have to try and get past that rock and as close as we can to the shore. It's our only chance," Sander replied bravely. He could feel the wind blowing his hair wildly.

They pulled dead even with the rocks and were only about a half dozen yards away. They could see sheets of spray flying into the air as the river drove wave after wave hard against the stone. Above Satan's Toes rose the implacable fortress of the Dunderburg. The lowering sky pressed down until the mountain was lost in its dreary shrouds. The tide was carrying them northward toward the cove, but it was still hidden beyond the impassable barrier before them.

Satan's Big Toe loomed up, full six feet above the waterline and sticking out the length of the long-boat into the water ahead. The waves churned over the smooth surface of the stone. The boys and Alfar had only the barest hope of clearing the tip, avoiding certain destruction, and making it to the safety of the cove that lay beyond.

Alfar threw the tiller over hard to port, and the longboat finally responded, turning sideways to the rock and facing back out toward the river from the shore. Sander and Bobby pressed hard against the oars, and the boat inched ahead until they were halfway round parallel to the shore.

Sander, looking over his shoulder, could just glimpse the sheltered cove. Another stroke would do it. They would be in the clear. At the last moment a fierce wind howled down the mountain and tore at them. Sander felt the oar being torn from his hand. A huge wave lifted the longboat into the air. He saw Bobby tumble and Alfar fly backward over the stern as the boat was hurled violently onto the projecting rock.

He felt the dull thud as the boat struck the rock sideways. At first it was like a distant explosion, a cannon fired off in the distance. Perhaps DeVries was signaling. And then the explosion reached him. The longboat was wracked from stem to stern, and his whole world became a crashing, rending sound as the boat was torn asunder.

Sander dimly saw the shattered boards flying into the air as he went tumbling along with them. Water was everywhere. He tried to breathe, but all was wet and tumult. He was desperate for air. He tried to claw his way back to the surface. He didn't know if he was swimming up or down. He finally broke the surface and gasped, filling his lungs. He couldn't see what had happened to Alfar or Bobby.

Pieces of the longboat were careening off the rock with the action of the waves. The sky was black with rain. He felt himself raised up by another wave and was about to be dashed against the rocks as the longboat had been a moment before. Then something struck him in the head, and everything went black.

CHAPTER THIRTEEN

Sander felt himself being dragged ashore on his stomach by the Goat-boy and the dwarf. His rescuers collapsed in the sandy mud of the beach, and Sander knew that they must have somehow reached the cove. His head hurt from the blow he had received, and he felt as if he had swallowed the river. He coughed up what seemed like gallons of water from his stomach. He figured he must have been hit on the head by a flying timber. Bobby the Goat-boy and Alfar were also the worse for wear. Bobby had a big bruise on his shoulder from a collision with debris. Alfar had a nasty swelling knot on his head as well.

The fury of the storm had abated, and the veil over the river had lifted. The little sloop was gone without a trace, and Sander had no way of knowing if it had survived the storm. Then he realized that survival meant a repetition of the same terrible event, day after day. Their mission came back to him in a flash, and his head cleared. Mini, DeVries, and perhaps even the Hessian still remained victims of Dwerg's tyranny. Their freedom was entirely dependent on him. But having borne the brunt of Dwerg's power, he was finding victory even more remote. Sander felt for his backpack. The weapons DeVries had given him were still there.

Soaked to the skin, they sought shelter farther up the cove. A gentle foothill curved around the tidal inlet. The hill was dotted with boulders and covered with thick undergrowth and small clinging trees. Fresh water spilled down from a cleft in the rocks to mingle with the salty inflow. The mountain itself was ringed with a full-grown forest, a wall of stout oak and maple. Above the tree line were sheer cliffs of granite.

The trio climbed a short rise and rested under a larch to gather their strength. They tried to eat a bite of Sander's olykoeks, but they were soaked. The pork tasted of salt water. They drank a little fresh water instead. Alfar studied their surroundings until he got his bearings.

The three adventurers were deep in the forest of Dunderburg Mountain. This was Dwerg's domain, where only the lost or the foolish would trespass. The trees rose thick and dark above them. Only sporadic flashes of sunlight told them it was still daytime.

Following Alfar, Sander had no idea what direction they were heading, except that they were moving toward the summit. He and Bobby did their best to keep up. The little man bounded ahead of them, drawing on seemingly endless reservoirs of energy until the boys begged for a rest.

"Alfar," Sander asked, beginning the question that had been forming in the back of his mind. He took the time to compose it carefully, so as not to offend the little man. "I've been thinking. It's too much to ask of you to refuse your grandfather's wishes. It's not fair to put it all on you. And it's not going to work anymore to just say no anyway. Things have gone too far now for that. Wouldn't it be easier if we just snuck in and stole Mini back? We could hide her somewhere where he can't find her, and maybe he'll forget the whole thing."

Alfar cocked his head and looked at Sander thoughtfully. Sander could see that the little man's feelings were hurt. Bobby looked from one to the other, not following.

"Look, Alfar, it's nothing against you, but Dwerg's too powerful. How could you resist him face-to-face? You never have. And your own powers aren't fully developed yet. We have to come up with another way to free Mini."

"Didn't think much of my hound, eh?" the little man said to Sander, sounding disappointed. "Or was it the funny animals that came after? I thought they were almost mythological." He gave a little snort that could have been fighting back tears.

Sander didn't like the way this was going.

"Maybe Alfar just has to catch Dwerg at the right time," said Bobby, trying to find a compromise. Sander shot him a look. Alfar got slowly to his feet to stretch his short legs. He stood over the two boys, and Sander could hear him heave a huge sigh. He cracked his knuckles.

"Okay," Bobby said, eyeing the dwarf and scrambling for a safe middle position. "Say we sneak in and wait for the right moment . . . "

"But how are we going to sneak into the Great

Hall without Dwerg catching on?" Sander interrupted. "That's what we should be planning now."

The two boys looked crossly at each other, frustrated at this rupture in their alliance and unable to find a way back to the good feelings they had shared earlier in the journey. There was a strange sound from somewhere behind them, the crack of a twig and then a sudden rush like air being let out of a balloon. They turned, and Alfar was gone.

"Alfar," Sander called, "I'm sorry. Come back." But there was no answer.

"Now look what you've done, Sander," Bobby said accusingly. "We're lost in the middle of the woods with our guide gone. We're a million miles from home, wherever that is. We're right under the Lord of the Mountain's nose. And he's still got Mini. Jeez," Bobby finished in genuine disgust. "What are we going to do now?"

Sander held his head. Boy, did that go wrong. All he had wanted to do was get Alfar off the hook for something he could never pull off anyway, and now look what had happened. He still believed they would have to find another way. Only now he and Bobby were going to have to do it on their own. Sander stood up and looked around the clearing.

"C'mon, Goat-boy, let's go." He stooped to pick up his things. He unzipped the backpack and dropped the canteen inside. He slung the pack across his back, adjusted the bow, and tightened the makeshift quiver holding the arrows.

"Where?" Bobby asked.

"Up the mountain, just like before."

"By ourselves?" Bobby asked, his forehead crinkling. "What the heck can we do?"

"For now, climb," Sander answered. "For the rest, we'll see." He smiled at Bobby and gave him a good-natured punch on the arm. "I messed up, Bobby. What can I say? Sorry."

Bobby shrugged his shoulders and got to his feet.

"I feel sorry for Alfar," Bobby said. "Having no father and a grandfather like *that!*"

"Me too," Sander agreed. "Now get those hooves of yours moving."

Up and up they climbed. The forest never thinned, and the way grew steeper. The woods were strangely silent now. There was not even so much as a bird cry, and Sander felt they were being watched. The hairs on the back of his neck rose, but he pushed on. Occasionally he thought he heard the sound of softly padding footsteps. Once, he was sure he caught a glimpse of something moving off to the side of their path. He dismissed his fear. Of course, there would be animals about. They were, after all, in the woods.

He turned to see how Bobby was doing. As soon as they reached the wall at the base of the cliff, he planned to let Bobby pick the rest of their route. The Goat-boy would know better how to traverse the rocky slopes leading to the top.

Sander soon realized that they would not make the base of the cliff by nightfall. The forest was dark to begin with, and they were moving east to north. The sun had long passed over, and they were in the shadow of Dunderburg Mountain. They were going to have to find a spot to make camp soon and light a fire. They would have to scale the mountain tomorrow.

Before long they came to a sheltered area where a group of large granite boulders lay scattered among the trees, the result of a rockfall eons ago. Here there was plenty of kindling to make a fire. The two boys made camp against one of the bigger stones. They gathered wood, and Sander opened a small plastic container. Inside, protected by a layer of wax paper, was a handful of kitchen matches.

They had survived the dunking.

"Gee, and I thought we were going to have to rub sticks together," Bobby said, laughing as Sander struck a match and lit the blaze. The fire burned merrily and cast a cheery glow around the two boys, huddled together under the hulking wall of stone. They felt hungry now, but there was nothing to eat but a fistful of nuts and berries they had gathered on the lower slopes during their climb.

Before long they both fell asleep. The fire burned low. Several hours went by until suddenly Sander woke and sat up. The hair on his arms prickled. Something was close by. The fire was almost out, and there were only a few shafts of moonlight that pierced the dark canopy of the forest overhead.

Sander squinted and saw a shape detach itself from the shadows. It was low and swayed slightly from side to side as it moved. It was circling the perimeter. A second shape was approaching from the opposite side. Both flanks were covered, and he and Bobby literally had their backs to the wall. Sander assumed there might be other animals hiding in the darkness as well. He nudged Bobby quickly and reached for his flashlight. He was glad he had remembered to replace the batteries.

Bobby rolled over and rubbed his eyes.

"Wake up, Bobby. We have visitors," Sander whispered.

Bobby was wide-awake in an instant. He grabbed his slingshot and picked up a stone from a pile of chestnut-sized pieces he had piled next to him. Before he had gone to sleep and while there was still light enough to see, he had carefully gathered a number of the same-sized stones, great for hurling, he'd said. Sander had prepared a pile of pine boughs dripping with sap. If there was going to be a fight, he and Bobby would need more light to see their targets. He had no doubt that sharp animal eyes were easily boring in on him right now. It seemed like the animals were waiting to spring, but he couldn't imagine what was holding them back. He felt for his bow and arrows next to him.

"Ready?" he asked Bobby.

"All set," Bobby replied.

Sander tossed the first pine bough onto the fire. It would take a moment to catch, and in that moment Sander would shine his flashlight into their assailant's eyes just long enough to blind the attacker and for Bobby to get off a stone from his slingshot. If that didn't scare them off, as soon as the bough flared, he would be able to shoot arrows from the bow.

He picked up the flashlight and aimed it where he had last seen some movement. He clicked it on, and a bright beam stabbed out across the uneven ground in front of the boulder and up against a bush at the foot of a large oak tree. There was nothing there.

"Darn," said Sander, and swung his beam. A large gray wolf stood staring at them with big yellow-green eyes blinking into the bright light. The wolf's mouth was open, with lips curled back to show a row of sharp teeth.

Bobby instinctively fired his stone, and the stone found its mark. The wolf cried out in pain as Sander switched off the light.

"Where's the other wolf?" Sander rasped in a violent whisper. He pointed the flashlight where he had last seen the second shape and turned it on. The wolf was still there, crouched and wary after its partner's outcry.

"Shoot," Sander urged, and Bobby's slingshot fired a second time. This shot went awry, and the boys saw the wolf jump away into the bushes before Sander turned off the flashlight.

"We need more light. What's the matter with the fire?" Bobby asked urgently.

"The bough's not caught," Sander said.

The air was becoming smoky. The fire was still smoldering, but the stubborn pine refused to flame.

"Light it again," Bobby insisted.

"I put the matches down somewhere," Sander said, worried now that their defense was about to collapse.

There was a snapping sound off to their left. Sander shot the beam of light once again. There were two wolves now where the first had been. Bobby fired. There was a thunk and a yelp, and the beam went off.

Sander's eyes adjusted to the dark once again. He heard Bobby's voice next to him. "Are they together now, or is that another one?"

"I think that's a new one," Sander guessed.

"Great," Bobby said, disheartened. "I wish we could see."

At that moment the pine bough flared up. The light flickered wildly over the rocks and trees around them. What it revealed was not three wolves but six, and Sander thought he could make out still more pairs of yellow-green glowing eyes.

"A pack," he exclaimed.

Bobby started firing as fast as he could with his slingshot. "Shoot, for crying out loud, Sander, shoot!" he yelled.

Sander grabbed for his fairy bow and set his first

arrow. He pulled back and let it fly just as one of the wolves was about to charge. The arrow sang a beautiful high-pitched musical note, clear and strong, as it shot across the clearing. It pierced the wolf's chest, and it dropped in its tracks. Sander felt a rush of elation. The fire dimmed momentarily, and Sander quickly threw on another bough as Bobby continued his hail of stones.

The bombardment and the sudden, unexpected fairy bolt cowed the wolves momentarily. The boys took advantage and pressed their attack. Sander's arrows felled another wolf and wounded yet another in the flank. The second bough caught, and the fire rose higher than before, casting an eerie, quavering light over the scene. The wolves were howling now, a terrible sound.

"Yippee," Bobby squealed with excitement. "We'll have them on the run in a minute, Sander."

Sander felt the giddy rush of victory rising in him. His scalp tingled and his ears burned.

Sander threw another bough on the fire and the fire rose higher still. Then the boys saw to their horror that the wolves were being joined by others of their tribe, who slowly emerged from the shadows. There were now more than a dozen, tongues out, lolling, saliva dripping from their fangs. Their collective growl was like the rumbling of a thunderstorm growing closer and closer. Sander and Bobby were ringed by the entire pack of fierce gray wolves, lean and gaunt and angry.

"Jeez, Sander," Bobby exclaimed, "I'm almost out of stones."

"I don't have enough arrows, either," Sander said, his heart sinking.

The circle of wolves drew closer. Sander threw the last bough on the fire. "This is it," he said grimly. He and Bobby squeezed one another's hands briefly to shore up their courage to face the end. Torn to pieces by wolves. Sander was momentarily grateful that at least his parents would never know what had happened to him.

The wolves crouched, getting ready to spring. The last bough flared up with a crackling rush as the rich sap took flame. It sputtered into a fierce blaze. At that moment the first wolf broke the circle and rushed at them, leaping. Midair, it stopped as if it had hit a stone wall. There was the sound of steel and a wound ripped the side of the wolf open. It lay on the ground, bleeding, chest heaving, and then was still.

"What the . . . ?" Bobby said.

The boys didn't have time to think. The pack rushed them all at once. Sander got off two quick shots and two wolves fell. Bobby fired off the rest of his stones in quick succession. He was deadly accurate with his slingshot. One, two, three wolves were struck. Two went down, with the third wounded. But the invisible warrior took the most terrible toll. The leaping wolves were caught, hacked, and tossed in the air by a powerful, unseen force. Their bodies lay heaped in a ring near the fire.

Sander had his next-to-last arrow slung when one of the wolves broke through. He felt the weight of the animal knocking him back, pressing on his shoulders. On his back, he felt the stones poking him and the animal's hot breath in his face, the teeth going for his throat. Then the weight was suddenly yanked from his chest. He saw the wolf flung through the air by an unseen hand. It struck against a tree with a terrible crack. The wolf fell to the ground dead, its back broken. The last of the pack fled into the bushes and disappeared.

Breathing hard, Bobby and Sander lay back against the stone and stared blankly at the fallen wolves.

"Are you all right?" Sander asked.

"Yeah," Bobby answered numbly. "I'm in one piece. You?"

"A little beat up, but I'm okay," Sander answered, still panting from the fight.

"What *was* that thing?" Bobby asked, struggling to find words for the unseen warrior.

"I don't know, but I think he's still here," Sander replied. As if in response to his words, an armful of brush was swept up at the foot of the trees. The two boys watched in amazement as the brush floated over to the fire and fell on it. The boys gasped, unsure of what to expect next from their protector.

The fire roared up once again. Waves of heat shimmered up, and the trees on the other side of the fire seemed to quiver and undulate in the background. There was a disruption of the wavering light as if something were moving behind a veil, and in a twinkling Alfar appeared.

"Alfar!" Sander and Bobby exclaimed in unison.

The little dwarf stood before them, his hands readjusting his sword in his silver belt. He was smiling down on them.

"Did you miss me?" he asked with a gleam in his eye.

"Boy, did we ever," said Sander.

"Me too," echoed Bobby, and the two boys jumped to their feet and gave the little man their biggest hug. Alfar clasped them both, then held them at arm's length and regarded them apologetically.

"I was angry, Sander, so I left," Alfar said. "I started back down the mountain."

"I'm so sorry, Alfar. I never meant to hurt you. I shouldn't have said what I said."

Alfar waved him off. "But you were right. At least about one thing. My powers *are* underdeveloped. I was too embarrassed to admit it. I realized I couldn't abandon you, so I just shadowed you as you made your way up the mountain. The wolves sensed my presence, so they kept their distance for a while."

"But how did you make yourself invisible?" the Goat-boy asked.

Alfar explained about the silver belt that Dwerg had given him. He demonstrated the turning of the belt—disappeared, then reappeared again.

"Whoa, that's so cool," Bobby said admiringly.

"Pretty neat," Sander agreed. "But the belt doesn't explain how you came to be such a fierce fighter, Alfar."

Alfar nodded. "Maybe it's my Duergar blood after all," he said.

CHAPTER FOURTEEN

Invigorated by their baptism by fire and too excited to sleep, the reunited adventurers decided to set out for the base of the cliff, so as to be ready to scale it at first light. Each carrying a firebrand in one hand, armed with sword, slingshot, or arrow, the little band marched away from its recent battle-field. Walking by torchlight in the dark, they made slow passage through the woods. With determination they moved steadily, although until they actually touched the cold, hard face of the stone escarp-ment, they couldn't measure their progress.

After an hour or so Alfar, who was leading the way, raised his hand, and the trio halted in silence. Tall elms pressed close against the deer trail here, and they could see but a few yards ahead. The only sound was the burning of the torches, which they had replenished along the way. Alfar shook his head and was about to move on when the unmistakable sound of high-pitched voices came floating across the night air. Sander, Alfar, and Bobby could not believe their ears. Who could be in this desolate forest in the dead of night? And then, unbelieveably, they heard music.

They resumed their pace and pushed ahead toward the source of the music. As they drew closer, they could clearly distinguish the playing of pipes and fiddles. The deer trail opened into a path wide enough for two that wound up to the crest of a hill. A shimmering yellow glow could be seen through the trees, dancing above the crest. Sander could feel the stir of fright crawling up his back. Alfar had the boys extinguish their torches. There was no need for them now. Cautiously they edged up to the top of the rise.

The yellow glow came from a huge bonfire, which cast towering shadows on the rock face above. Circling around the fire, dancing to the music, was a band of strange creatures roughly the same size as the boys, but there the resemblance ended.

"The Duergar," Alfar said, spitting it out contemptuously. Their bodies were stocky and muscular, their skin was dark, their eyes an intense, deep hunter green. They wore green deerskin jerkins and brown leather boots and beautiful jewelry—rings and bracelets, necklaces and armbands of silver and gold. Most wore long gray beards. Their voices, which were high and musical, did not fit their squat, ugly figures. They sang a song in a language Sander could not understand.

"Black Dwarfs," said Sander slowly under his breath.

"But they don't look like you," Bobby observed, curious.

"My mother was a Brown Dwarf, to Grandfather's shame," Alfar explained. "Dwerg says my mixed birth is the source of all my shortcomings."

A lone elder tree stood beside the fire, and on a thick branch above the dance a great horned owl looked down upon the proceedings. On the far side of the bonfire was a gathering, which they could not make out for the flames.

Alfar pulled the boys back from the crest, and, out of sight, they plotted their next move.

"A gathering of the Duergar is very serious. Something must be going on, and we had better find out what it is. We should hide until first light. They can't be out at daybreak."

"We could circle along the edge of the woods until we can see what's on the other side of the fire," Sander suggested.

"We have to be extremely careful not to be seen," Alfar cautioned. "The Duergar are cruel and dangerous. They would not appreciate our barging into one of their secret gatherings."

"What would they do?" Sander asked.

"Pluck off your toes. Put out your eyes. Pile stones on you until you are crushed to death," Alfar said.

"That's disgusting," Bobby said.

"Hurts, too, I bet," Sander added.

"What about your belt?" Bobby asked. "Couldn't you just walk right in there without them ever knowing you were there?"

"Too risky," Alfar answered. "The Duergar are extremely sensitive to magic, particularly their own, and this belt came from Dwerg. They might not be able to see me right away, but they would know I was there. It would be like walking in ringing a bell. And once disturbed, they might hide, and we would learn nothing. Or they would capture us, and then . . ." He let the thought hang, then continued,

"Nothing we would learn would be of any use to us."

The threat sent shivers up Sander's spine.

"Let's do as Sander suggests," said Alfar, deciding. "We'll work our way around the line of trees until we can get a better look. But whatever you do, stay together. If we get separated, we're lost."

Remaining just within the edge of the forest, the three travelers picked their way slowly and carefully around the side of the grassy hollow. A half-moon and a clear night provided adequate light through the sparse vegetation. Making sure not to be seen, they gradually drew closer and closer to the imposing stone facade of the Dunderburg.

As Sander and his friends sidled through the forest, the celebration seemed to pick up in speed and intensity. The pipes grew shriller and the fiddling faster and faster. Sander cast a glance at the dancers. Their movements grew faster, in time with the music.

"If they did no worse than let you join them, you would dance for a year and a day," Alfar warned in a dark whisper. "And by then it would be too late."

They reached a secure spot abutting the cliff face. A line of trees descended along the mountain wall down to the bottom of the earthen bowl where the dancers remained light on their feet and as merry as ever. At the very base of the cliff, a spring flowed out of a cleft in the stone and a small stream wound through the hollow and disappeared into the woods.

A flat, grassy apron in front of the trees held a slight depression in the earth, affording them a full view of the gathering without being seen. Sander slung his bow across his back. They lay on their bellies and squirmed forward for a better look. Sander saw a large black willow tree growing alongside the little stream. It had several trunks, with upward sweeping curves. The willow's dark and heavily ridged bark rose into a dense treetop with an irregularly shaped crown. Sander's heart was beating hard. But it was not the closeness to the dancers that had set him off. Another vision had struck his eye.

The Duergar were celebrating a wedding feast. Beneath the enormous black willow tree a fairy banquet was set on a long wooden table. Laden with food and drink, the table was surrounded by guests. Sander could feel the Goat-boy poking him in the ribs with excitement.

"People! Nobody's piling rocks on them!" whispered Bobby.

"Quit it," Sander said.

"Hush," said Alfar harshly.

There were more than a dozen guests, including Indians and, from what Sander could make out of their garb, farmers of the Colonial period. They pressed close around a seated couple.

Suddenly Sander was gripped with fear. What if Dwerg had abandoned his plan and was marrying Mini to somebody other than Alfar? His stomach tied up in a knot. As if to confirm his suspicions, one of the guests moved aside and he could see the bride, radiant in a white gossamer gown. She had beautiful brown skin and high cheekbones. She was laughing, and the resemblance was unmistakable.

He could feel the ripple as the shock of recognition ran through Alfar and Bobby, lying next to him. A terrible sense of loss ran through him. He wanted to cry. Still, something about the situation was not quite right. Of course, he thought, she's under a spell. Nothing about this situation could be right. But then, at that moment of doubt, the guests stepped back, the couple rose, and Sander got his first good look at the groom. He was a smiling young man of German descent, dressed in the crisp, colorful uniform of a Hessian grenadier; a handsome soldier, sword dangling in its scabbard at his side. It was Josef Herder.

The truth struck Sander in the pit of his stomach. He felt a sense of giddy relief. The bride was not Mini at all. It was her great-great-great-great-grandmother, the daughter of DeVries and his "ochqueu," his woman, strangely reunited with her ghostly lover.

He watched as the wedding processional began. The Duergar had ceased their dancing. The pipes and fiddles fell silent. The Black Dwarfs lined up in two rows beneath the great horned owl on the branch of the lone elder tree. As if at an unseen signal, the wedding party moved toward the waiting Duergar. As they walked, a beautiful sound rang out through the hollow. It was the strumming of a harp. The notes floated on the night air and seemed to penetrate to the deepest part of Sander's brain, numbing him.

From behind the shifting figures, a voice began to sing a song of irretrievable loss, of a love that could never be regained. He recognized the voice at once. It belonged to Mini. And the song was "Woman of the Murmuring Sky"! The gay wedding party cleared from view, and then he saw her. She sat alone, playing the harp and singing beneath the black willow.

Before he knew what he was doing, Sander was

on his feet and running. Alfar whispered fiercely for the Goat-boy to stay put, and he leaped up and pursued Sander. Bobby took out his slingshot and craned his neck for a better view.

Sander, gripping his bow, had plunged into the line of trees that ran along the cliff face. Moving rapidly behind the thin screen of trees, he was already halfway down the slope that led to the little stream and the black willow tree where Mini was playing.

Chasing Sander, Alfar could see at a glance that the wedding was about to begin. The bride and groom strolled down the aisle formed by the Duergar toward the owl, who was ruffling his neck feathers.

Sander drew as close as he dared without leaving the cover of the trees. The group was standing in front of the elder tree and facing away from him, except for the owl, who appeared to be looking down at the bride and groom. Keeping the black willow between himself and the owl, Sander slipped out and ran across the open ground to Mini. He hid behind the three curving trunks of the black willow and called to her with a low whistle.

"Mini."

She moved very slowly, as if she were in a

dream. Her head turned and she noticed him, but she did not move from her place by the harp.

> *"In the land of the tall green willow,*
> *only listen for her sigh;*
> *like night's dark curtain falling,*
> *O woman of the murmuring sky,"*

she sang.

"You have to snap out of it and come with me," Sander said.

But Mini only continued her singing.

> *"Lovers fleeing the mountain's shadow,*
> *feel the Duergar curse draw near . . ."*

"Please, Mini," Sander implored. "Come away with me. This is our chance to get away."

> *". . . as Pyngyp's cliffs lie taunting,*
> *a soldier's fate is sealed by fear,"*

she went on, striking the harp strings and staring raptly at the wedding scene.

Alfar braved the open ground and caught up with Sander crouched against the dark, heavy trunk of the black willow. He could see Sander's mounting frustration. He feared the boy was about to run out and try to physically carry Mini away.

"Sander," he said forcefully, pulling the boy around and looking into his eyes. "She can't hear you."

"Oh, but she can," the boy protested.

Alfar insisted. "Yes, but you can't get through. She is under the Duergar spell. This wedding is her dream, her fantasy. To break it now would destroy her."

Sander looked at him, heartbroken. He was so close. But he realized Alfar was right.

"The only way to break the spell is to defeat Dwerg," Alfar continued. "And then all these ghosts—and Mini herself—will be set free. Now come on."

Sander watched sadly as Mini began to play again. Her eyes were filled with tears as she looked on the wedding once more. He could see the bride and groom pledging their vows beneath the elder tree. There was a chorus of high-pitched voices as the Duergar repeated each vow as it was spoken. The owl was speaking the ceremony in the same language Sander had heard earlier, an ancient tongue that he could not hope to understand. Unconsciously he stood up, preparing to leave. At that moment the owl paused suddenly in its recitation.

A thrill went though Sander. He had been spotted, and he knew it. The wedding party turned toward the source of the interruption.

"Oh no," said Alfar beside him.

They felt the owl's eyes burning into them from across the hollow.

"Run, Sander," Alfar urged. But it was too late.

The great horned owl rose up on a shimmering current of air. It flapped its huge wings and soared toward Sander and Alfar. Sander bolted toward Mini, his arms outstretched. A cry went up from the owl at the intruders. The sound grated against the enveloping quiet of the night. The owl's cry was echoed by the watching Duergar and rose to a shriek. Mini stood up. The harp fell over with a discordant, resounding crash amid a rising wave of protest. Mini screamed. Sander's head hurt horribly from the sound. He felt suddenly dizzy and fell to the ground. He could see the great horned owl above him.

The owl gave a great flap of its wings and floated higher, a magnificent black silhouette against the bright white light of the half-moon. Sander could see the owl's talons outstretched as if ready to strike. He rolled to one knee, took a deep breath, and without thinking nocked an arrow and let it fly at the owl. He was sure he had missed. But then the entire scene vanished with a roar. The Indian bride, the Hessian, the Duergar, the bonfire, the owl, Mini. All gone in an instant. Sander and Alfar were left alone, flat on their backs in the grassy hollow in the dark.

It seemed as if a long time passed before they were able to move or talk. Finally a light shone on them. It was Bobby, holding the flashlight from Sander's pack in one hand, his slingshot in the other.

"Are you guys all right?" he asked. "I was starting to worry about you."

Sander started to cry. Little snuffling sounds came out of him, and he was embarrassed.

"I was so close to her," he managed to get out.

"It's okay, Sander," Bobby reassured him, approaching and kneeling by his side. "It's not your fault."

"It's no one's fault," Alfar said. He surveyed the glen under the moonlight. Everything was still. "We're safe here now. Get some rest. We'll move at dawn."

Bobby tossed Sander his pack, which he took for a pillow. Bobby lay down next to him, and Alfar snuggled in as well. The three curled up under the black willow tree and fell into an exhausted and dreamless sleep.

CHAPTER FIFTEEN

Dawn broke with the mountain shrouded in fog and mist. The sun shone red in the watery light through the trees that rimmed the hollow. The adventurers woke up stiff and weary from their short sleep on the hard ground. The grass was damp from the dew, and Sander felt cold and wet. He was hungry and tired, and he wanted to go home. He would have given anything at that moment to be sitting in his warm kitchen at the breakfast table while his mother served up heaping platters of pancakes and sausages.

They rose and stretched and prepared for their ascent of the Dunderburg. Sander refilled his canteen from the little stream, Bobby picked some wild mushrooms, and they were ready to go. Alfar was staring toward the summit obscured by the lowering sky.

"Should burn off in an hour or so," Alfar said, referring to the ceiling of mist that wrapped the upper reaches. "Let's get going."

Sander slung his pack and his bow and remaining arrow on his back. They set off at a brisk pace toward the cliff, with Alfar in the lead. Between the trees there was a spot where the rock was split open. A series of simple hand- and footholds gave onto a ledge above. Once on the ledge, the party made a partial circuit of the base with relative ease. From that point on, however, the incline grew more sheer and the climbing more difficult for quite a distance up the mountain.

The fog had begun to lift, and the sun burned hot on Sander's skin. He could see that they still had a long way to go, and his arms and legs ached already. Alfar was very strong and never seemed winded. If he got too far ahead, he would stop and come back to help his young friends over any rough patches. Bobby too was tired, but he was older and stronger than Sander and more used to scrabbling around on rocky surfaces.

Little by little they made progress. At the

halfway point they reached a large rock outcropping with a flat top. They were several hundred feet up. They stopped to rest and share a drink of water from Sander's canteen. The sun was high. The mist was gone, and the view of the river valley was clear and surprisingly empty. There were no trains. No ship traffic on the river. No roads, no bridges. Just an uninterrupted stretch of the Hudson Highlands, the soft hummocks of green rising above the sweeping curve of the Mauritius. It was hard to imagine that only twenty-four hours earlier they had been in DeVries's ship, battling a ferocious storm. Right now there wasn't a cloud in the sky.

They drank their fill and resumed the climb. In a short while they found themselves at a difficult crossing. The path was narrow, the hillside was steep, and the drop onto the rocks below was very long.

Sander and Bobby were pressed against the cliff and working their way sideways. Alfar had disappeared around a curve ahead.

"Bobby," Sander called out to the stocky figure beside him, "are you all right?"

"As long as I don't breathe too deeply," Bobby answered, hugging the rough stone face.

The path seemed to be no wider than the length

of their sneakers. Sander could feel his heels pressing on nothing but air. As the path rose, his left foot started to slip on the crumbling surface. His heart began to race. He was afraid of losing his balance. He froze, holding his breath. He remembered what his father had told him and slowly exhaled. He could hear Alfar speak soothingly close by.

"Grab hold as tight as you can to those rocks above and carefully place your feet," Alfar coached. "Let your weight ease into each step. Feel the shift from one side to the other."

Sander took another breath, relaxed, and began to inch forward again.

The path widened slightly, and the footing became more secure. Sander glanced over his shoulder, and it was then that he saw the crows. A flock came wheeling around the mountain out of the east. Descending like a dark and threatening storm cloud, the crows dived at the climbers, attacking them as they clung to the side of the cliff.

But these were no ordinary crows. The birds weren't black at all. As they approached, Sander saw that they were colored a bright red, almost like parrots. They had three legs and sharp beaks. And the third leg had especially sharp claws.

The air was filled with streaks of red, raucous cawing, and the flapping of wings. Their cries redoubled, echoing off the stone walls of the Dunderburg. Sander felt the angry rush of beating wings. He could feel his back being raked by the sharp claws and the painful pecking of beaks on the back of his head. The birds were pulling at his hair, tearing at his skin.

"Cover your eyes," Alfar yelled. The crimson crows were trying to peck out their eyes and leave them blinded on the cliff. Sander took a hard peck over the right eyebrow and lashed out. He felt a satisfying solid connection with a feathery body and watched the crow bounce off the mountainside below.

Bobby screamed, and Sander looked over to see him fighting off several of the terrible birds with one arm while struggling to keep his balance and hang on with the other. Alfar edged up the incline, making room for Sander.

"Move up," he called to the boy, "move up."

Bobby found a foothold and, firmly wedged for a moment, began to pry small jagged pieces of shale loose and hurl them at the birds with his slingshot. Several birds were struck and instantly fell from the sky. Still, the climbers were severely outnumbered. And there was no escape from the naked cliff face. Only down.

Sander could do nothing. He couldn't bear the attack without at least trying to fight back. He turned sideways, pulled off his backpack, and, at the same time, slid his bow loose. He had only one arrow remaining, and he would need both hands. He let go of his backpack with the flashlight, canteen, and other gear and watched it drop hundreds of feet to the rocks below. The flat *thunk* of the backpack as it hit the rocks was so small and so distant, it sounded to Sander as if it were coming from another world.

He nocked the arrow to the bowstring and looked for a prime target. For a while he had the sense that one of the crows had held back from the actual attack and seemed almost to be directing it. The birds wheeled away from the cliff again and took formation for a final assault that would sweep the boys and Alfar off the side of the mountain. It was then that he saw the leader, away to one side. This bird was slightly larger and older-looking than the others. He flapped his wings with a certain authority, and when he cawed, Sander imagined that he could hear the other birds answering.

The leader was cawing angrily now at the flock, as if urging them on to the attack. Sander took careful aim, pulled back on the string, and loosed the arrow. It sang a clear, high, warbling note as it flew with deadly accuracy toward its target. The arrow struck the big red crow, piercing his breast and coming partway out his back. He hung in the air there for a terrible moment, his cry choked off. He sunk, tried to flap his wings, but his heart had stopped. He began to drop, holding his wings outstretched and circling as he fell, until finally his crimson wings collapsed and he dropped like a stone onto the rocks at the bottom of the cliff.

The flock poised for the final attack, uncertain about what to do. There were still many more birds than the climbers could hope to vanquish, yet leaderless, the flock chose to run. With a tremendous rush of wind, they swooped up and around, sweeping in formation close by the trio clinging to the narrow path. And then the flock rose until it was only a dark spot in the sky above and disappeared.

With the retreat of the red crows, the remainder of the climb was uneventful. The trio arrived near the top of the northeast face in the late afternoon as the shadows were deepening. They were on the upper rim of the Dunderburg now, a slight incline where a piece of the mountain had sheared off in an ice age eons ago. Massive boulders were heaped up, and the spaces between them seemed to offer several different avenues to pursue.

"There are many blind alleys," Alfar said, sorting out the best choice. "It's been a long time."

"What do you mean?" Sander asked.

"I was never allowed to play on this side of the mountain when I was a kid. My mother was afraid I would fall. So I spent most of my time on the southwestern slope, which has a much gentler grade."

"So where are we heading now?" Bobby asked.

"To find my secret entrance," Alfar said.

"There's another way into the Great Hall?" Sander said.

Alfar nodded. "I found a hole that let out onto the top of the mountain," he said. "It was my little escape hatch when I needed to get away from the rantings of my grandfather. But the way to the top is hidden in this maze of rocks."

The little man's eyes searched the boulders until he got his bearings. "Follow me," he said, pointing to one of the many stone corridors. "We've got to find the entrance before nightfall. We don't want to be out on the mountaintop after dark. Who knows what animals Dwerg will have patrolling here for his protection?"

The little man led the boys into the stone alley. The boulders rose high on either side until there was only a narrow strip of blue sky above. They clambered over the rubble of smaller stones that littered the path as they continued up the incline. The path wound among the boulders, twisting and turning. At intervals, several smaller forks presented themselves, and each time Alfar had to make another choice. Three times his choice led to a dead end and the expedition had to work its way back to the intersection and try again.

It was twilight. The tops of the boulders were turning red-orange with the setting sun, and the pale-white blank of the moon hung in the darkening sky above them. They turned a corner and the branch opened up before them. It ended in a steep slope of loose stone that led to the very top of the mountain. There was no way up.

They turned to retrace their steps yet again and found, to their dismay, that two powerful-looking, woolly goats with long, spiraling horns blocked the path. The goats bent their heads and displayed the sharp tips of their horns threateningly. The little trio started to back up toward the slope. Sander looked over his shoulder to calculate the difficulties of trying to outrun the goats up the rock-strewn slope. He saw three more of the mean-looking goats appear over the top. Their escape, if it could have worked at all, was blocked. They were surrounded.

There was the sound of metal sliding on metal as Alfar drew his sword from his silver belt. He stood crouched in a fighting position, arms extended, one holding the sword, the other in a fist.

"Back-to-back, boys," Alfar said with grim determination. Sander picked up a heavy stone and hefted it, readying for a throw.

"Your slingshot, Bobby," Sander said.

"We're not going to need it," Bobby answered slowly. Sander was facing the slope, and he could see the goats on the rocks above. They appeared to be conferring. He looked past Alfar and Bobby, who were facing the way they had come. The other two goats raised their heads expectantly. One came slowly forward but bent his head again.

For a moment, Sander feared he was going to ram Bobby. But then he simply placed his head against Bobby and nuzzled him like a dog. Bobby put his hand out and patted the goat on the neck.

"They know you!" Sander exclaimed. "But they can't be from the herd at Goat's Walk," he said, puzzled.

"Your reputation precedes you, Goat-boy," Alfar observed with a twinkle in his eye. He put his sword back in his belt. Sander dropped the stone.

The goats helped to push the trio up the slope of loose stone to the very top of Dunderburg Mountain. No matter how much they might slip and lose their footing, the goats held firm and pushed from behind. The other goats waited patiently above. As the climbers neared the top, the goats bent their heads, dug in, and offered their horns as a secure grip. The climbers grabbed hold and pulled themselves up.

At last the adventurers stepped up onto the great stone dome of the Dunderburg. It was like standing on top of the world, with a three hundred and sixty degree view of the pristine Mauritius River valley. The sun was down, the sky shot through with its fading brilliance. To the west lay a crimson blaze. To the east, the purpling night sky, dotted with a few pale white clouds, stretched to extinguish the light. Overhead, the first stars were coming out.

Alfar searched the surface in agitation, looking for the long-lost escape hatch that led back to his childhood home. The goats milled around Bobby as he helped Alfar. Finally a cry went up from Alfar. He had found it.

The light was fading quickly now, and Sander regretted the loss of his flashlight, which had fallen with his backpack down the side of the mountain during the battle with the red crows. He could see a small natural crevice that hid a hole in the dome. The hole led into blackness, so Sander had no idea of how long a drop lay beneath. Alfar explained that he used to have a rope to slide down onto a rocky shelf below. From the shelf, he would lower himself further onto a stack of stores kept in a little-used hallway. The hallway led to another corridor that eventually ended in the throne room of the Great Hall. Dwerg's bedchamber lay just behind the throne room.

Alfar decided that, without a rope, they would have to form a human ladder to descend into the cavern. The goats stood in a circle and locked horns above the hole. Bobby straddled the hole, feet spread wide apart while gripping the goats' horns. The plan called for Sander to hold on to Bobby's legs and slide down into the hole as far as he could go. Alfar, since he had the most experience, would then climb down over Sander and drop onto the narrow rocky ledge below. Once Alfar touched down, Sander would stand on his shoulders while Bobby climbed over both of them. Sander would then jump off and all three would be on the interior ledge.

Sander felt the dwarf's weight as Alfar climbed over him. Alfar did his best to move quickly without jostling or poking Sander so he wouldn't lose his grip, but the strain was telling. Sander clutched Bobby's legs hard, and he could feel the boy working to hold on to the goats' horns. Suddenly Sander felt Alfar's weight release, and he knew that he was down. Bobby groaned with relief.

"I'm on the shelf," Alfar whispered upward from the darkness within. "My shoulders are a few inches below you, Sander. You're going to have to extend your feet as far as you can, and then let go. I'll be there to help you balance the moment you touch my shoulders. When you hit, reach out—the wall will be about eighteen inches in front of you."

For Sander, this was an act of faith. From somewhere in the near distance, he thought, came the light tinkling sound of a bell. He wondered briefly as he looked up at Bobby and the goats framed against the twilight sky. Sander stretched his feet, let go, and dropped into the black hole. He felt Alfar's shoulders and reached instinctively for the wall. His hands felt the hard stone surface in the dark, and he recovered his balance. He stood swaying lightly on the little man's shoulders, and looked up the shaft toward Bobby.

"Bobby," Sander called quietly. "C'mon, you're next."

Sander could hear Bobby exclaiming up above. "Heather," he said.

Heather's bell. The thought raced through Sander's mind. Bobby's lost kid from Goat's Walk. What could she be doing here?

"It can't be," Sander said.

"C'mon, Goat-boy, let's go," Alfar said in a gruff tone, not hearing what Bobby had said. "We can't waste a minute."

The bell tinkled again clearly now and moved closer.

"Heather," Bobby said again. "She's here. I have to find her."

"No, Bobby, don't," Sander called to him. "C'mon, your turn, let's go."

He could hear the bell moving away now and jingling rapidly, as if the little goat were running. He heard the scrape of Bobby's footsteps as he pulled himself out of the crevice to pursue her.

"Bobby!" Sander cried, helplessly.

"What's going on?" Alfar growled. Sander's weight was starting to press heavily on him in the dark. He lost his balance. Alfar swayed, and Sander caught himself on the wall. He jumped down, and he and Alfar stood side by side on the shelf in the dark.

"Bobby's gone," Sander said with sad finality.

"Oh, no," Alfar said.

The two stared up at the hole in the ceiling. All they could see was a faint patch of blue-black sky as night fell. No goats. And no Bobby.

They turned to each other in the dark. "What could have happened?" Sander asked. Alfar shrugged and turned up his palms in a helpless gesture.

"I don't know."

The two stood in silence for a brief moment,

and then something came hurtling down savagely through the hole in the roof above. It jangled metallically against the stone and bounced to Sander's feet. He bent over and picked it up. It was Heather's bell. Alfar reached out with one hand and stifled the clapper so as not to make another sound.

"C'mon," he said. "It's just us now. Let's go."

CHAPTER SIXTEEN

Numbly, Sander wrapped Heather's bell in his handkerchief, unwilling to let go of this totem of the lost Goat-boy. He stuck it in his pocket and looked around him. His eyes were adjusting to the light, and he realized that there was a torch burning somewhere in the outer corridor that enabled them to see a few mostly shadowy outlines. He and Alfar moved along the ledge until they came to the stack of stores that Alfar had remembered. They climbed down carefully over the boxes and made their way toward the light. At the door to the corridor they paused. They waited for what seemed like hours to make sure that Dwerg was asleep and all was quiet in the Great Hall before they made their move.

They had reached the moment of truth. Sander

had in mind a plan to propose to Alfar. Stammering under his breath, he managed to get it out:

"Alfar, I have an idea. As long as the Duergar have Mini, we can't hope to free her until we find a way to weaken Dwerg's magic. And if we can, he just might be willing to negotiate."

"But how?" Alfar protested.

"By stealing his magic cloak." Sander said boldly.

"What?" Alfar said in disbelief. "His cloak? Impossible. He hangs it on a hook in the throne room right outside his bedchamber, to guard him."

"That doesn't sound so difficult," Sander said.

"More than you know," Alfar said, and told him about the wight in Dwerg's cloak. "He never sleeps. And he has a very bad attitude."

"What if one were to sneak up on him wearing Silverstorm?"

"The wight knows me, and he would know a dwarf was there before I could get my hands on him. Just like with the Duergar. Invisible or not."

"What if it wasn't a dwarf who was wearing the belt, but a boy?"

Sander asked this in his most innocent tone, not wanting to be refused. He desperately wanted to persuade Alfar that this was the best course of action. He was sure Dwerg would collapse at the loss of his favorite talisman. If only Alfar would believe him. He strained to read the little man's expression in the dark. Alfar turned his baseball cap all the way around and tugged on the brim three times, which meant that he was thinking.

"You? I don't know. It would be very dangerous."

Sander felt elated. Alfar was considering it.

"What would you put him in?" the dwarf asked.

Sander looked around him quickly. On the floor, next to some crates of sugar and coffee, he spied an old flour tin, a tall can about twelve inches high and six inches on a side. He picked it up and dumped the contents out on the floor. "What about this? I'll stuff him in this tin, and I'll hold the lid down tight."

"And what am I supposed to do while all this is going on?" Alfar asked.

"This is the best part," Sander said mischievously. "You're going to take the wight's place."

"But I've only ever done animals. I don't know if I can transform into a wight," Alfar said, sounding more than a little worried.

"Well of course you're not going to be a real wight," Sander argued. "But can't you conjure yourself up as a fake cloak to fool Dwerg if he pokes his head in before I get away?"

"I suppose I could. There's an old trick called 'glamour,' in which the viewer is enchanted into believing you are whatever you want them to believe. You hardly ever see it anymore. It's mostly done at parties. I don't know if Dwerg would fall for it, but he might if he wasn't expecting it and didn't look too closely."

"Well, can't you just transform into something that looks like Dwerg's cloak?" Sander asked.

"I could try," Alfar responded.

"All right," Sander said, hitching up his pants. "Let's go."

Reluctantly Alfar took off the silver belt and handed it to Sander, who slipped it around his waist.

"Just be careful," Alfar warned. "Silverstorm takes a little getting used to."

Sander put on the little silver belt with the shimmering scales. It fit perfectly. He gave Alfar the thumbs-up sign, grabbed the belt, gave it a twist and turned it around backward. There was that funny hissing sound like air let out of a balloon. Otherwise he wouldn't have known he was invisible. He looked at Alfar, who was looking at him strangely. Sander took a step toward him and fell on top of him. Alfar caught him and stood him upright.

"See what I mean?"

Sander nodded his head but realized Alfar couldn't see him.

"Yes," he whispered.

Sander looked down at his arms. He couldn't see them. Or his legs. Or any part of himself. It made him dizzy. He looked around him. Something was wrong. Even in the dim light everything looked distorted. He remembered trying his father's glasses on once and how crazy they'd made everything look. He almost fallen over then, too.

"Wow." Sander gave an involuntary sigh, and then collected himself. He picked up the flour tin, which looked as if it had floated off the ground and disappeared beneath his shirt. "Let's go."

"Wait a minute," Alfar said. "I can't just go waltzing in there with you."

"Well, think of something," Sander said, "something small that won't be noticed."

"Oh, that's easy enough," the dwarf answered in a hushed voice. He turned his hat around, held his arms wide, shook himself, and, before Sander's eyes, turned himself into a little brown mouse. He wiggled his whiskers, started for the door, then stopped. He wrinkled his nose, turned around, and looked longingly at the piles of food stores.

"Gee, I hate to leave all this," he said in a high, squeaky voice. "Couldn't we have a quick snack?"

"Later," Sander answered as if talking to a small child. "Now c'mon."

Alfar scurried through the slightly cracked door and into the corridor. Sander slowly opened the door and followed.

To an observer, the sight of a little brown mouse hurrying along a wall would invite no surprise, particularly in a cavern as large and complex as the Great Hall of Dunderburg. There were plenty of mice, a few rats, bats, spiders, and snakes already living here. One more wouldn't attract any notice. The only odd thing about this mouse was a strange seam in the air that appeared to follow along behind it. The seam created only the slightest distortion in the visual field as it moved, like a ripple across the surface of a still pond.

To Sander, of course, the corridor, lit by torches on the walls, looked positively weird. This must be how fish see things, he thought. The walls curved upward on either side of him, with only the center in focus. Sander felt slightly nauseated. The flickering torchlight sent shadows wriggling across the ceiling and floor that only made his stomach feel worse. He imagined how weird it would look if he were to suddenly throw up.

Putting one foot in front of the other, and holding on to the wall for balance, Sander quickly got used to the look of things from the perspective of the invisible. They had reached the end of the corridor, and the little mouse had stopped at an entrance. He cautiously peeked around the corner, then quickly pulled himself back and pressed close against the wall. Sander reached down and picked Alfar up. He could feel the little mouse's heart pounding and his breath coming in short spurts.

"That's the trouble with being a mouse," Alfar managed to whisper. "Great scouting, but fear is magnified a thousand times."

"Okay," Sander said, "relax. Everything's going to be okay. Now, where's that darned wight?"

"We're just outside the throne room. Dwerg's bedchamber is on the other side, and the cloak is hanging on the wall just outside the door."

"All right," said Sander, steeling himself, "follow me." He put the mouse back down on the floor and started to turn the corner and enter the throne room.

"How can I follow you if I can't see you?" the little mouse whispered.

"Count to three and then go in," Sander replied. "I'll go on two and be just ahead of you. As soon as I've grabbed the cloak off the wall, you jump on. Got it?"

"Got it," the mouse answered.

Sander entered the throne room. The high ceiling soared above. A fire burned low in the stone fireplace. The flat stone Dwerg used as a throne was empty. Sander could see a closed door across the hall that must lead to Dwerg's bedchamber. Hanging on the wall outside the door was the wight. Sander could hear him talking to himself in wight gibberish.

"Gone are the bones of the Darmagh. Full night do the moonbeams glow. Deep in the marches they'll find you. If ever the sly wheel go. One turn to the Hesperides. And then to the island mill. Where the maelstrom flows full circle. And the pounding blood goes still," the wight said.

Sander ignored the wight's ramblings and crept closer and closer to Dwerg's door. He passed the throne at mid room and turned to check on Alfar. The mouse was moving along behind him. He stopped to sniff at crumbs on the floor and ate a few. Whether he was hungry or just trying to act like a mouse, Sander didn't know. He realized that Alfar shouldn't get too close or the wight might get suspicious.

To his relief, he saw the mouse stop again and make a meal of some cheese that had fallen from the Lord of the Mountain's wooden table. Alfar busied himself around the table leg, gathering more scraps. Sander tiptoed closer to the cloak until he was almost upon it. The wight had stopped chattering and hung silently, just within reach. His black folds were draped over a wooden hook. Sander could see the threads. His hand reached out toward the cloak.

"Oh, my little skillywidden," the wight said suddenly, breaking his silence. "Come to take us for a walk? A little outing perhaps?" Sander froze. He realized that the wight was no longer talking gibberish. He was speaking directly to him. He looked back to Alfar. The little mouse's back was turned, although his head was up and Sander was sure he was listening. There wasn't a moment to lose.

Quick as a flash Sander snatched the cloak from the hook and popped open the flour tin.

"Oh, we're going to make a cake?" the wight said.

Sander stuffed the wight inside and clapped on the lid as the wight waged a furious protest. There was the sound of stirring from Dwerg's bedchamber.

"Hey. No. Let me go. You forgot the eggs."

The flour tin, which appeared to be floating in the air, began to quake.

"Quick, Alfar. Now," Sander said.

The little mouse took off and ran for the wall. Sander wrestled the shaking flour tin halfway back across the throne room toward the fireplace. The wight's muffled cries could be heard rattling against the sides. The lid popped up momentarily, and Sander gave the tin a mighty swat, driving the lid down until the tin was shut tight. The wight made a swooning sound, and the struggle was over.

At that moment Dwerg's door flew open. The mouse made a leap for the hook and began to transform. Dwerg stood in the doorway in his nightshirt, looking irritable and holding a candle. He had somehow managed to pull his boots on. Fortunately he wasn't awake enough to see Sander tuck the tin inside the hearth by the glowing embers. Sander looked over at Dwerg and was horrified by what he saw. Dwerg was much taller than he expected. But that wasn't what bothered him.

There, not five feet away from Dwerg, was Alfar, in full view as himself, a dwarf dangling from the wooden hook by his shirt collar. He gave a little shrug, as if he had felt Sander's startled glare.

"What's all the racket?" Dwerg said, addressing the wight but still looking straight ahead. He hadn't noticed yet.

"Nothing doing here, boss," Alfar answered in his best wight-as-cloak voice. He took off his red baseball cap and stuffed it in his pocket.

"The devil you say," Dwerg said, turning toward Alfar at the exact moment the little dwarf finally transformed. Alfar's cloak was a little disheveled and threadbare, but in the poor light Dwerg might mistake it. Sander caught himself as he began to breathe a sigh of relief, afraid that Dwerg might hear him.

"I didn't say anything about the devil," Alfar said. Sander wished Alfar would stop talking—he was only digging himself into a deeper hole.

"What's the matter with you?" Dwerg asked.

"Nothing wrong with me. I'm fit as a fiddle," Alfar the cloak said. As if to demonstrate, he flew up off the hook and across the room. Alfar was unused to the shape, so his flight left quite a bit to be desired. He looked like he was about to crash at any moment. He cartwheeled across the throne and rushed past the stunned Sander. He almost flew into the fire but made a last-moment course correction and rocketed up to the ceiling. Dwerg looked on his antics with disapproval.

"Have you gone bats?" Dwerg asked.

"Bats," Alfar exclaimed. "I can do bats."

Alfar transformed into a huge bat and dropped from the ceiling, suspended in front of Dwerg.

"Bats, hats, cats," Alfar said, transforming into each in turn. A succession of hats was replaced with a huge frizzy black cat. He stood in front of Dwerg, his back arched and hissing. Sander suddenly realized that Alfar had so distracted Dwerg that it was the perfect time for him to get away with the real wight trapped in the tin.

He turned back to the hearth and reached for the tin, but the wight had begun to stir.

"Whew," the wight said in a very faint, tinny voice. "Miami sure is hot this time of year."

"Rats. How about rats?" Alfar continued, turning into a giant rat standing up on his rear legs, baring his teeth.

Sander snatched up the tin and was about to

stick it under his shirt. It was hot. He hesitated for a brief moment, bobbling the tin on his fingertips.

"Enough," boomed Dwerg, exasperated, in a voice that filled the hall. Alfar froze, transformed back into a cloak, and wrapped himself around Dwerg, as he had seen the wight do so many times.

"Sorry, boss," he cooed, settling down like a dog on a rug. Dwerg shrugged his shoulders, adjusting to the strange movement. Clearly Alfar's cloak didn't feel right to him. It wasn't what he was used to. Dwerg walked over to the throne and sat down uncomfortably. He had yet to notice the tin bouncing up and down in midair by the fireplace beside him.

"Ahh, ahh, ahh," the wight said.

Oh no, Sander realized. The wight was going to sneeze.

"Ahhhhchooo." The wight sneezed and blew the lid right off the tin. He was out in a flash. The tin lid clattered against the stone floor. Dwerg looked up with a start.

"Look at me," the wight said in an angry voice. The black cloak floated in midair and was streaked white with flour. "I'm a filthy mess."

Sander wanted to run, but he couldn't leave Alfar stranded around Dwerg's neck. The wight began flipping around in the air, trying to shake off the flour. The air was filled with fine white dust. Sander's invisible face was beginning to be faintly outlined in white. His nose began to itch too. The wight spotted Alfar, cozily ensconced around Dwerg's shoulders.

"Hey," he said to the fake cloak. "That's my spot."

"Who does he think he's talking to?" Alfar asked with false bravado.

"Oh," Dwerg said with an evil smile. "Someone's up to a bit of trickery, is he?"

"Achooo," Sander said, his invisible sneeze making a very audible sound. Dwerg's head came around in an instant. He looked at the spot where the sneeze had come from and quickly sized up the situation.

"A man can always use another good cloak," he said to no one in particular, reaching up to his chest and fingering the cloth. "If it's made of the right stuff."

In a flash, he snapped Alfar from around his neck, hurled the cloak to the ground, and stamped his boot on it. The wight, wasting not a moment, flew to his master and took up his customary place across his shoulders. He preened like a bird.

"Oooh, poor little barn brownie," he said, gloating at Alfar's misfortune.

"Unfortunately," Dwerg continued, as Alfar flapped around helplessly under his foot, "it looks like someone is trying to pass off shoddy goods."

Sander lost it. The empty flour tin clattered to the ground as Sander rushed Dwerg.

"Let him go, you big bully," yelled Sander with vehemence, shoving Dwerg. In all his many years as the Lord of the Mountain, no one had ever laid hands on Dwerg. He was caught completely off guard by Sander's physical assault.

Stunned by his invisible attacker, Dwerg fell to the floor with a thud. Sander, carried by his own momentum, tumbled over Dwerg and hit his head hard on the stone floor. The silver belt was inadvertently turned around in the melee, and Sander rolled to a sitting position in plain sight, holding his aching skull.

Alfar, meanwhile, had slipped out from under Dwerg's boot and taken flight. The wight, seeing his master downed, flew up in a rage. The two cloaks hung there, facing off in midair. The wight transformed into a firedrake, a fiery spirit that twisted in the air like a snake. It hissed and curled, then struck in a bolt of flame as Alfar, as the cloak, jumped back.

Sander, looking on, couldn't restrain himself.

"Alfar," he cried, "you must change. Think of a fiend."

Alfar's cloak whirled and he was transformed into a hideous water bogle, dripping wet and covered with green slime and seashells that clattered as he waved his arms. He clasped the firedrake and extinguished it in a cloud of steam and smoke.

The steam and smoke were sucked back into Dwerg's cloak as the wight escaped from Alfar's water-bogle embrace. The wight soared again into the air and became a kind of kelpie. The demon had the body of a horse but webbed feet. Its head was like that of a Chinese dragon, with a short snout, short horns, fierce, red eyes, and sharp, protruding teeth. Giant wings like a bat grew out of its back. Its long mane was mired in a clutch of green rushes. The kelpie gave a great snort and leaped onto the water bogle's back, crushing him down under its great weight.

Then Alfar's water bogle rose up as a hideous troll, a misshapen giant with a club who tossed the kelpie away as if it were a sack of grain. The kelpie became a black boggart with the head and body of a dog, saucer eyes, huge padded feet, and the tail of a scorpion. Alfar turned into a magnificent

229

griffin, a four-footed beast with the head of a leopard, the tusks of a boar, the beak, body, and wings of an eagle, and the hind end of a serpent.

The battle raged on, wight against dwarf, in a succession of guises. Each time Alfar bettered the wight, Sander would cheer. Dwerg, who had regained his seat on the throne, glared malevolently in his direction. Unaware that he was no longer invisible, Sander stuck his tongue out at Dwerg.

Alfar, struggling with the wight, saw Sander on the floor out of the corner of his eye. His tongue was still out, and Sander was putting his thumbs in his ears and waggling his fingers at Dwerg.

"Sander," he yelled, jabbing his finger in Dwerg's direction. "He can see you."

Sander stared back at Alfar without realizing the import of what he said. He was in awe of Alfar's performance. Dwerg, meanwhile, was smiling evilly right at him.

The wight took the opportunity of Alfar's distraction to become old Raw-head Bloodybones, a horrible specter from the pit, dripping in blood and wielding fistfuls of raw bones. It landed a mighty blow on Alfar's crown, staggering him.

Alfar reeled, then came back as Redcap, a

malignant old man with blood-matted hair, fiery-red eyes, long, pointy teeth, claw hands, and a grisly expression. Redcap swung an iron pikestaff to counter the blows of old Raw-head bloodybones. With awesome strength he delivered a final smashing blow that sent the wight scurrying back to his master like a whipped dog. The cloak wrapped himself securely around Dwerg's neck, and Dwerg stroked the wight as if he were an injured pet.

Alfar transformed himself back into a cloak and struck a triumphant pose as if with folded arms. "I guess that'll show who holds the mantle of King Goldmar around here," said Alfar, trying to keep up the pretense.

The hall was filled with the sound of slow, methodical clapping as Dwerg sarcastically applauded Alfar's victory.

"Alfar, Alfar, Alfar, how I've missed you," Dwerg said. "You have grown since I saw you last."

Alfar's cloak collapsed on the floor and Alfar stood meekly in his place. Dwerg wagged his finger at his errant grandson.

"You've been practicing, haven't you?" Dwerg asked in his most condescending voice. "And by Goldmar, you are good, too. Just as I always knew you would be." Dwerg sounded almost proud.

"And I bet your little friend here has been help-ing you." Dwerg turned his gaze on Sander, who realized, for the first time, that he was no longer invisible. He froze in terror. Dwerg laughed and slipped off the throne. He began to pace the floor between Sander and Alfar menacingly. Sander got to his feet and slowly began to edge his way back toward the entrance to the throne room and the corridor to freedom beyond.

"Why, he's even wearing the belt I gave you. My Silverstorm. You shouldn't be so careless with family heirlooms, Alfar." Dwerg gestured, and the belt flew off Sander's waist, spinning him in circles. Silverstorm wrapped itself around Dwerg's arm, then slithered around his trunk and down to the floor, where it coiled itself, hissing like a snake.

"But I thought you made it for me," Alfar said.

"I've never really been that good with my hands," Dwerg countered. "And after all," he con-tinued gently, "some of these precious objects have been with the Duergar for centuries." Dwerg paused. "Like my cloak, for instance. Which came from none other than King Goldmar himself."

Dwerg spit it out in a cold fury. "And you let Silverstorm be worn by a mere mortal?"

Alfar shrunk back. Dwerg changed his tone abruptly. He lowered his voice and appeared conciliatory once again. "But I understand. You're still young." Dwerg shot a glance back at Sander, who stopped in his tracks and appeared to be studying the wall hangings; then the dwarf continued. "You've discovered new powers, and naturally you want to try yourself against the old man."

Dwerg smiled, and Alfar winced as if he were about to be slapped.

"Well, so be it, then," Dwerg said suddenly. He tore off his cloak and flung it over Sander, ten feet away. Sander struggled for a brief moment. The cloak settled slowly to the ground, collapsing onto thin air. There was nothing underneath it. Sander had disappeared. Alfar stared in horror. The cloak lay heaped on the floor and Sander was gone.

"Never fear," Dwerg said. He stepped over to the cloak and whistled. The cloak leaped up and wrapped itself around him once more. Dwerg reached down and scooped up something in the palm of his hand. He held it out toward Alfar.

"I am not without compassion," Dwerg said. In

his palm stood a miniature Sander, shrunk down like a tiny Tom Thumb, waving his arms at Alfar.

Sander fell down on the palm of Dwerg's hand. His skin was rough—hard and scaly. Dwerg's voice boomed down at him as if it were coming from a thundercloud. "And I have plans for your young friend here," Dwerg said.

Dwerg took a step, and Sander felt as if he were riding on a moving mountain. Sprawled on Dwerg's palm, he held on to the horn of a callus to keep from sliding off. Dwerg was taking him to the far side of the throne room.

The wall opposite the throne was draped with a purple curtain, which Dwerg yanked aside. There, on a long, low stone shelf set into the wall, were four glass dioramas. Each glass contained a world of its own, with earth and sky and water. Sander's mind was fuzzy with shock and fatigue. He didn't realize what he was looking at, and then it hit him. The fairy worlds.

There, behind the glass, was the flat, silver-gray plane of the Mauritius, the sloop, and the gathering storm. He could see DeVries on the quarterdeck, yelling at his men as the black storm came sweeping down the mountain to engulf him and his ship.

There was the young Hessian racing through the woods, the Indians at his heels, the cliff of Pyngyp looming above him. There was sad Mini sitting beneath the black willow tree, plucking on the strings of the harp and singing her sad song. And Bobby. There was Bobby calling after Heather. His voice echoed dully against the enigmatic stone recesses of the implacable Dunderburg as he searched desperately for his lost kid.

Dwerg took another step toward the dioramas, and Sander, clutching at the Mountain Lord's palm, imagined absurdly how fascinating all this would be to his father. Mini's diorama loomed before him, a glass wall now obscured by a thick fog swirling inside. Sander knew this glass prison was to be his new home. Dwerg was going to seal him forever in this living nightmare—the dark vision of the Lord of the Mountain—trapped with the girl he had come to free.

Sander tried to make out the scene behind the glass as he felt himself being lowered into the fog. He was blinded. There was a roaring sound and a burning, choking sensation in his throat and chest. Sander couldn't breathe. And then Sander found himself once again on the slopes of the hollow at the foot of the Dunderburg.

As if in a dream, he walked slowly down the hill toward the wedding feast below. The great horned owl spoke in the indecipherable ancient tongue. The bride and groom pledged their vows beneath the elder tree as he had seen them do only the night before. The high-pitched voices of the Duergar chanted each vow as it was spoken. And through it all, Sander heard Mini's voice lifted in her haunting song. His spirits sank yet again as they had then, this time weighted down with the knowledge that he too was frozen in an endless loop of time.

The harp strings vibrated, and Mini's voice rang out clear and strong as she told the young lovers' tale.

Sander thought of his father and his fondness for the strange voices of the past. Unconsciously he reached in his pocket and felt the matchbox tin. He felt its age and solidity and the gentle rattling of the bead. And then he remembered his father's advice. He stopped in his tracks and breathed a deep breath, drawing in a chestful of mountain air, fresh and cool.

He began, surprisingly, to sing. It was as if his voice were rising from somewhere outside himself. A thrill went through Sander.

"Lovers fleeing the mountain's shadow
feel the Duergar curse draw near;
as Pyngyp's cliffs lie taunting,
a soldier's fate is sealed by fear."

Sander sang.

The owl paused at this stupendous interruption. The wedding party turned toward Sander, singing beneath the black willow next to Mini.

Mini smiled, and she and Sander sang the final verse together: He had no idea how he knew the words, but he felt his breast swelling with the song.

"The Black Dwarf struck and now he holds her,
in the fairy world gone by,
but never doubt her heart's true longing,
O woman of the murmuring sky."

Sander reached his hand out to Mini, and she took it.

"Mini," Sander said.

"Sander, where am I?" Mini said.

At that moment Sander heard a thin cracking sound, like a skin of ice breaking on a pond. The sound, like shattering glass, increased in volume,

237

then rose to an earsplitting crescendo. Sander watched in amazement as, behind the row of Duergar and wedding guests, the walls of the mountain seemed to fragment and break apart, falling in glassy shards. He saw crazy reflections of the owl fluttering upward from its perch, the Duergar drawing their daggers, the fire leaping free of its bounds, the guests scattering, the Hessian and his bride hugging each other in close protection.

It was as if a giant's sword blade had cleaved Sander's world in two. Fragments of the wedding feast seemed to spin lazily in the air. The wedding guests turned to face the destruction and screamed at the terrible figure they saw: A gigantic gray squirrel was sticking its nose into the hollow, shrouded in flying glass. Its nose was wiggling.

"Sander," the squirrel said. "Quick, jump on and let's get out of here."

It was Alfar, just like the night in Sander's attic. Sander wasted no time.

"I'll explain later," he said to a dumbfounded Mini. "C'mon."

He grabbed Mini's hand, and the two leaped onto the squirrel's back, Mini in front. Alfar charged straight back through the still-flying shards of mountain, trees, and smoke from the spreading fire. Sander looked over his shoulder. The Duergar were fleeing, the owl flying at their head. He could hear the screams of the cowering wedding guests.

The smoke from the diorama spilled into the throne room as the squirrel hit the floor. They could hear Dwerg yelling furiously to the wight as Alfar raced into the stone corridor that led to the entrance to the Great Hall and the slopes of the Dunderburg beyond.

Alfar was moving fast. Sander and Mini clung to his fur and buried their faces in the back of his neck, holding on for dear life. Sander could feel the squirrel's muscles gathering under him as he raced toward fresh air and freedom. He peeked upward as the glimmering light from the torches in the sconces far above him turned the shaft into an eerie scene. The pocked granite wall of the cavern seemed to fly past.

Then Sander heard a shrill cry coming from behind him, from somewhere deep in the shaft below. The cry turned to a shriek, and a chill went up Sander's spine. Dwerg was coming. And he was very upset.

The screech owl flew close to the ceiling of the corridor above the torches. He looked down, his sharp eyes piercing the shadowy light. He scoured the granite floor, with its rock outcroppings and debris piles of wood and stone, looking for his prey. He knew every nook and cranny, and to his mind there was no hiding place that he could not penetrate. He flexed his powerful claws and flapped his wings, driving harder.

Sander could feel a current of fresh air on his face. They must be nearing the top. Alfar's pace had never slackened. He was running full out, and Sander could hear his breath coming in short, panting spurts. But Alfar didn't seem to tire, and the squirrel ran as if his little heart would burst. The corridor began to widen, and for the first time Sander felt a ray of hope. Their escape was at hand.

They reached the outer chamber leading to the mouth of the cave. The floor widened into darkness as they left the torches behind. Alfar seemed to know where he was going and didn't miss a step. Sander strained to see in the darkness. He thought he discerned the outline of an arched opening ahead of them. There was just the faint trace of light within the frame, where the blackness of the cavern walls shaded into the deep purple of the night sky outside the mouth of the Great Hall. Sander realized it must be almost dawn. The screech owl struck.

Sander felt the wind rushing from the beating of wings above. The owl's sharp cry exploded in his ears and made his head hurt. He ducked down instinctively and tried to bury himself further in the squirrel's fur. He felt Mini flinch and duck as well, as Alfar shifted his direction abruptly to evade the owl's attack. Sander judged they were still headed for the archway into the mouth of the cave. There was nothing he could do in his present tiny size but hold on to the back of the squirrel as hard as he could and pray for Alfar to escape.

He could hear the fierce clicking of the squirrel's nails as they scratched across the stone surface to the mouth of the cave. Sander knew that once there, the owl would have even more room to maneuver. Yet he still hoped that somehow they would find a place to hide.

The screech owl swooped down on them in a series of attacks. Each time, Alfar swerved at the last minute and just managed to evade the grip of those terrible claws. But each change of direction cost them precious time. Their path became a chain of zigzags across the cave floor, littered with centuries of stinking debris. Blood, bones, and the slimy muck of animal remains were piled high everywhere. Sander's nostrils were filled with the rotting stench of death and decay. They trampled skeletons, dodged behind stones, and ducked under tumbled boards in their race for freedom.

At last they raced under the final archway and through the door into the yawning mouth of the cave. Sander could see the remaining stars glinting faintly in the night sky. The waning moon hung outside the opening like a silent celestial witness to the harrowing chase. He could breathe deeply of the fresh air and the breeze blowing up the river to sweep the mountain clean. Then he heard the beating of the owl's wings once more, closer than ever. Mini screamed a high, piercing scream, and Sander suddenly felt himself caught in the pincer grip of those sharp claws as he was ripped from the squirrel's back. He felt himself, to his horror, being drawn upward. He could see Mini's terrified, upturned gaze. The squirrel ran around in agitated circles. Sander was caught again. And this time there would be no reprieve.

There was a flutter as the owl settled onto the stone floor and a swoosh as he became Dwerg again, swathed in his magic cloak. Sander felt himself held tightly in that horny palm, and his whole body went slack. He was completely and utterly defeated. He bit his lip, forcing back tears.

There was a second swoosh as the squirrel returned to the shape of Alfar. He hung his head dejectedly. Tiny Mini leaped up onto a rock so she was as high as Alfar's knee.

"Sander," she called.

"I'm all right," he squeaked.

"Congratulations, Alfar," Dwerg said. "Your training is almost complete. You are truly ready to become a full-fledged Black Dwarf, your parentage notwithstanding. All that remains is a simple act of will. You must choose to become one, just like me."

"And what of my friends Sander and Mini, and the others?"

Dwerg laughed horribly. "What of them?"

"Will they go free?" Alfar asked.

Dwerg laughed again. "I leave that up to you. Their fate is in your hands. Though be warned, once you are anointed as a Duergar, you may feel differently toward them than you do right now. So choose your fate, Alfar. What's it going to be? Black Dwarf or a brief, unhappy life of great insignificance?"

Sander could see Alfar struggling. He thought of Bobby and Mini and DeVries and the Hessian.

And of Alfar, standing there, contemplating giving himself up to a life that he dreaded and abhorred.

"No," Sander said, his voice sounding thin and small in the darkness.

He felt Dwerg's grip tighten, squeezing the life out of him. But he couldn't stop now. Even if he were to be crushed, Sander had to go on. He breathed as deeply as he could.

"Alfar, where's your hat?" Sander yelled. Alfar stared at him dumbly. What in the world could he be talking about?

"Where's your hat?" Sander repeated. Alfar stuck his hand in his back pocket mechanically and fished out his red baseball cap.

Sander could hear Dwerg growling. He brought his fist up to his mouth. He grimaced at Sander, and for a terrible moment Sander thought he was going to bite his head off.

"Put it on, Alfar," screamed Mini. "Put it on."

Alfar did so, moving like an automaton. Alfar stood there with his red baseball cap on, not knowing what to do next.

"There, that's who you are," Sander called out to him. "A guy in a red baseball hat. And baseball can't be bad. Baseball is good."

Alfar tugged on the brim of his hat the way he

always did when he was thinking.

"You're not a Black Dwarf. You're a helper," Mini chimed in. "You helped me. You can't be someone you're not."

Dwerg's temper flared, and he snatched her up swiftly with his free hand. Mini shrieked.

"Be quiet, you little fool"—Dwerg glowered down at her—"or I'll turn you into a toadstool and stick you on that wall for a thousand years as a monument to your own stupidity."

"Hey, leave her alone," Sander said, struggling against Dwerg's grip. He pressed on, remembering what DeVries had told them on the boat. "Your father, Alfar. Remember what he did to your father."

"What?" Dwerg said angrily. "He knows all about how the Indians killed his father."

"That isn't true," Alfar broke in, finally finding his own voice.

"Of course it's true," Dwerg insisted, and for the first time Sander realized that Dwerg had told this lie so many times that he had come to believe it himself.

"Show him, Alfar," Sander screamed.

"Show him," Mini echoed.

It was still dark. From the shelf of the cave, the river could be faintly seen in the distance. Broken clouds were mounting up to hide the moon and deepen the shadows. Alfar stood against the sky and gestured with his arm. He conjured a vision of the night long ago when his father perished in the fierce Atlantic storm on DeVries's boat.

The wind howled, and they found themselves on the deck of a ship tossing in a stormy sea at night. Sander smelled the salty air and tasted the spray of the sea as it foamed over the wooden decks. He could feel Dwerg tense as the scene unfolded.

Belowdecks the boat rocked back and forth mercilessly in the enormous seas. Alfar's mother lay on a table, in great pain with the delivery of Alfar. Dwerg argued with a younger dwarf, who looked a lot like Alfar and whom Sander took to be his father, Rahbad. Rahbad was imploring his father to do something, but Dwerg was obviously filled with trepidation.

Sander remembered what DeVries had said about the ship's doctor. Rahbad wanted Dwerg to get DeVries to send the ship's doctor to help his wife. But Dwerg refused. He said he couldn't risk discovery by the ship's crew, who would mutiny if they knew dwarfs were aboard. But clearly something else was amiss. Sander saw something in Dwerg's face that he had never seen before—fear.

Rahbad kissed his wife and left the cabin angrily. Dwerg glowered and did nothing to comfort his daughter-in-law. On deck, Rahbad struggled to work his way down the heaving deck. Sea after sea crashed down over him as he progressed slowly toward DeVries, who was strapped to the helm. Despite the fierce gale and the gigantic foam-flecked seas that inundated the ship, Rahbad still managed to cling to the rail. Little by little he drew closer to the quarterdeck and the captain straining at the helm.

Sander could feel Dwerg's distress growing as the scene progressed. His palms started to sweat, and Sander could feel the moisture creeping into his clothes. At the same time, Dwerg was reflexively tightening his grip and Sander could hardly breathe. Sander remembered the sheer animal panic he'd felt when he had first fallen into the snake pit. He was registering that same kind of feeling from Dwerg now.

Sander forced himself to watch Rahbad. Alfar could not bring himself to look. Behind Rahbad, from the opposite side, an enormous rogue wave raised its head, towering above the ship. The wave crashed over the stricken vessel, and for a moment she simply vanished beneath the tons of ocean water that cascaded over her. Then the wave passed on. DeVries struggled to regain his balance and gripped the helm once again. But the deck was empty and Alfar's father, Rahbad, was gone.

Sander could hear Dwerg suck in his breath at the terrible sight. For the briefest of moments he almost felt sympathy for this dark creature who had lost his only son. But Alfar interrupted Sander's thought. His voice quavered in quiet fury.

"You lied to me," he said to his grandfather.

"No," Dwerg protested weakly.

"You lied to cover your own shame."

"No" was all Dwerg could say in reply. "It's not true."

"But why?" asked Alfar. "Why? He was your only son. Why wouldn't you help him and my mother?"

Sander could feel a shiver go through Dwerg, and the Mountain Lord momentarily relaxed his grip. Sander gasped for air and yelled into the darkness.

"Because he's a coward," Sander cried. "Admit it, Dwerg. You were afraid."

"No," Dwerg mumbled, weakening further.

"Afraid?" said Alfar, uncomprehending.

"That's right," Sander said, driving it home. "He's afraid of the water."

The statement was like a stone hurled against

Dwerg's temple. He reeled and then caught himself. Dwerg was terrified of water. Where most dwarfs simply didn't like it, he was literally paralyzed with fear. But the Atlantic crossing was years ago. He had survived intact. Or so he told himself.

"No," Dwerg said hoarsely, refusing to submit to the truth. "Your father was headstrong. Just like you. He was willing to risk everything and expose us. He could have continued my legacy. He was a fool. He destroyed my dream."

"And it cost him his life," whispered Alfar sadly.

Sander was outraged. "You know what your problem is, Dwerg?" he snorted. "It isn't that you're heartless, it's just that you have a heart of stone."

At Sander's words Dwerg's head went up. He craned his head slowly and studied the dwindling night sky as it gradually gave way to the coming dawn.

"It's a trick, isn't it?" he muttered craftily. "Keeping me out here with your windy stories. You're stalling until first light strikes."

"First light? What's he talking about, Alfar?" Sander cried.

"It's the oldest law," Alfar answered. "A Black Dwarf caught out at first light turns to stone."

Dwerg glared at his grandson. "But you would

be caught too. You would sacrifice yourself to destroy me?"

"A small price to pay," Alfar replied, "if it were true."

Dwerg raised his two arms above his head as if to dash Sander and Mini against the cliffs below. "I'll set a price," he threatened.

Alfar flinched. "No, don't," he said, surrendering at last. He heaved a sigh. "I'll do what you ask. I'll become a Black Dwarf." His head went down in shame.

"No, Alfar," Sander and Mini exclaimed simultaneously.

Dwerg lowered his arms to his sides, and Sander and Mini exchanged breathless glances.

"Then let's get below before it's too late," Dwerg said.

As he spoke, there was a low rumbling sound as a stone door in the archway at the rear of the cave mouth began to close. It slid with a low growl over the narrow opening to the tunnel that led back down into the bowels of the Dunderburg. Dwerg stepped inside the archway as Alfar followed, his head bowed.

Sander watched the slowly grinding wall of stone, the torches flickering in the tunnel ahead, all with the piercing clarity of a condemned man being led to the scaffold. He felt Dwerg's grip relax and realized numbly that Dwerg had finally won. The knowledge went through him like a knife. He felt desperately alone.

"Miniiiiiiiii!" The cry sprang out from the depths of his twelve-year-old soul.

Mini, in Dwerg's other hand, bit down firmly onto a loose patch of skin between Dwerg's thumb and forefinger. With a sudden cry of unexpected pain, Dwerg's body jerked, both his hands opened reflexively, and in an instant both Mini and Sander had fallen to the ground.

Mini stumbled and fell flat. Sander rolled to his feet and ran instinctively toward the shrinking opening as the sliding stone door ground slowly on to seal them forever in the mountain.

"Sander!" Alfar and Mini called after him. But it was no use. He was through the opening, and he knew exactly what he had to do.

Out of the corner of his eye he saw a snapshot of the scene behind him. Mini had hurt her leg in the fall, and Alfar was helping her to her feet. Dwerg, enraged again, had turned toward the fleeing Sander but hesitated at the threshold. The door was almost shut. Dwerg raised his fist in fury.

Sander quickly raced the short distance to the lip of the cave. He judged the angle of the mouth to the sky and pulled the Hessian's match tin from his pocket as he ran. Despite all the time he and his father had spent looking at the heavens, he realized he knew very little about the morning sky. Yet his very life and the lives of his friends depended on his being right.

He had noticed the faint line, like a hairline crack, that had appeared in the sky as Dwerg had held him fast. He figured that the mouth of the cave faced slightly to the southeast and calculated that therefore first light would break to his left.

"You dratted little elf," Dwerg's voice rasped behind him.

Sander sensed the door behind him was about to close. With a desperate rush, he leaped forward, arms outstretched as far as he could reach. He held out the tin matchbox, its polished surface giving off a dull shine.

The first light of dawn broke the horizon. A single shaft rent the heavens. Sander seemed suspended in space. The beam struck Sander's outstretched hand, bounced off the match tin, and flashed back straight at Dwerg.

A gasp went through Dwerg as he saw the light coming for him. The sunbeam lanced him through the heart, and he shuddered as Sander dropped precipitously over the edge of the cliff.

"Sander!" Mini cried, but her voice was lost in a sudden deep rumble from the mountain.

The earth began to shake violently. A tremendous quaking seemed to spring from the deepest roots of the mountain. The stone door shattered and fell in pieces, exposing the open mouth of the cave. Mini and Alfar were swaying. And something strange was happening to Dwerg.

Alfar stared at his grandfather, his eyes widening.

"First light," Dwerg said, shaking his head in disbelief. "How could it be?"

Mini stared in amazement at Dwerg's legs. His leather boots were stiffening and turning gray. Ridges appeared where there had been grain, and their suppleness turned to a rocklike solidity. Dwerg looked down in horror at what was happening to him. Gray veins were creeping up his legs. His legs began to swell, and the huge marbled veins seemed to be growing out of the mountain itself.

Dwerg moaned and his eyes glowed with a green fire.

"What's happening?" shrieked Mini at Alfar above the grinding, crunching din. The little man stood watching in stunned silence.

Dwerg poked his forefinger toward Alfar as the creaking, crackling veins of granite continued to course up his body. "But you. Why not you?" he croaked.

"I'm a Brown Dwarf, remember? You always told me so. No good Duergar blood here. Blame my mother," Alfar said.

"Sander!" Mini screamed suddenly, realizing he was nowhere to be seen. "Where's Sander?"

A small, muffled voice came from over the edge of the cliff. "Help me, please, someone." It was Sander. All that could be seen of him were his hands gripping the ledge. Dwerg's spell on him broken, he had returned to full size. He was dangling over the cliff, his body weight pulling him down toward the rocks far below.

The sound of Sander's voice propelled Dwerg into one final cataclysmic effort of his dark will. Dwerg raised one thick stone leg and set it down with a heavy thunk. He raised the other and, wobbling, set it down with a crunch in front of the first. Only the deepest Duergar malevolence carried him forward. Each thunderous step grew heavier and more laborious than the one before, as Dwerg advanced in a slow, crushing stagger toward Sander, who hung on perilously to the rocky ledge at the mouth of the cave.

Tiny Mini grabbed Alfar's pant leg. "C'mon," she said. "Quickly." She hung on as the little dwarf dashed across the stone floor to lift Sander free before Dwerg could reach him.

Mini and Alfar bent over the ledge and tried to ignore the dizzying heights below. Sander looked up at them, pale and frightened. He held the matchbox tin in his teeth. Alfar reached down and grabbed hold of Sander's arms. Mini was still too small to be of any use. She jumped up and down, urging Alfar on as Dwerg drew nearer.

Dwerg, his thickening arms outstretched, continued his inexorable march. He had turned a terrible shade of gray. His green eyes burned. Flecks of mica shone on what used to be his skin.

Sander, his breath coming in furious bursts between his clenched teeth, dug his fingers into the stone. He saw his friends above him and felt Alfar's grip on his arms, lifting him to safety.

The stony figure of Dwerg loomed above them,

his face contorted with rage. Dwerg reached out in hatred toward Sander as Alfar helped him scramble back up onto the ledge. The three collapsed at Dwerg's feet. Arms like tombstones began to reach slowly down for Sander as the final change came over Dwerg. There was a great crackling sound as the spreading rock gripped the Lord of the Mountain, entwining his torso in sheets of stone.

Dwerg, almost immobile, felt his fate penetrate his soul. He rotated his hands, cupping them instead, and bent toward his grandson, imploring.

"Please, help me," Dwerg whispered. Those were his final words.

Dwerg froze in the pose of supplication toward Alfar. His cupped palms were raised to the sky, beseeching. His face was completely gray, his skin turned cold and hard. They gasped at the sight.

The sun broke the horizon fully now, and light streamed through the clouds across the river. It reflected off the inner mouth of the cavern and cast a rose-gold hue on the Dunderburg, on Sander, Mini, and Alfar, and on the still, stone figure of Dwerg.

Mini returned to her normal size with a rush and fell at Sander's feet. He helped her up and they marveled at the sight of Dwerg, who had finally assured the permanence of his legacy, though not exactly in the way he had planned.

The Lord of the Dunderburg had turned completely to stone.

CHAPTER SEVENTEEN

A sweet wind blew over the Hudson Highlands. Like a sigh of relief, the breeze swept across the forests of the Dunderburg and out over the Mauritius, the great river glistening in the afternoon sun.

Alfar held court in the hollow at the foot of the mountain, the red baseball cap pulled down tightly on his head. His ragged Bible wedged firmly in his back pocket, Alfar perched regally on a three-legged wooden stool by the black willow where Mini had played her harp. He smiled a lopsided dwarf grin at the gathering throng before him and clapped his hands in time with the music.

A celebration was underway. DeVries and his prosthetic pirates had been transformed and made whole once again. Gone were the hooks, eye patches, and wooden legs. The sailors danced a lively horn-pipe beneath the trees. The reunited lovers, the Hessian and Mini's great-great-great-great-grand-mother, danced along as well, joined by all the members of their wedding party.

On the rise above, a ring of curious forest ani-mals looked on. Deer, fox, possum, and hare stood side by side, staring. The tree branches dipped and swayed with the shifting of the hundreds of robins, red-breasted nuthatches, and grosbeaks gathered there. Their song mingled with the shrill piping and fiddling below.

A small procession wound ceremoniously through the crowd toward Alfar. Mini walked at the head, bearing a garland of wildflowers. At her throat was the necklace of crimson bone that had belonged to her great-great-great-great-grandmother, with the missing bead returned to its rightful place. Sander marched at her side, with the once-lost Bobby trailing behind. Heather, her bell jingling, followed Bobby the Goat-boy to bring up the rear.

The three friends stood before Alfar. A hush fell over the hollow. Only the breeze stirred. Sander was the first to speak, his strong young voice rising to be heard by the full assembly.

"Alfar. Friend and magician. You have demonstrated extraordinary wisdom and self-sacrifice. You have acted in the spirit of natural law. You have established your powers beyond a shadow of a doubt. The dominion of the Mauritius and the Hudson Highlands is yours to rule in harmony and justice."

Sander motioned to Mini, who stepped forward and raised the garland high for all to see. Alfar looked up in wonder at the garland suspended above his head. Sander gave him a nudge.

"Take off your hat," he whispered.

Alfar removed his red baseball cap. Mini gracefully placed the garland on Alfar's brow.

"You are hereby declared the new Lord of the Dunderburg," she said.

A cheer went up from the crowd, and Alfar rose to his feet and bowed deeply. He waved the gathering to silence.

"Thank you all. In honor of this sacred month, let us begin the feast of Haleg-monath with a special celebration. For I decree that Josef Herder will finally be joined with his Indian bride, O buh bau mwa wa ge zhig o qua," Alfar said, pronouncing the Algonquin for "Woman of the Murmuring Sky" perfectly. The two lovers embraced, then hugged Sander and Mini.

And so Josef Herder, son of turf cutters from Germany, reluctant grenadier, and lover of an Indian girl from the New World, was married at last to the great and only love of his life. Many shed a few tears at the sweetness of it, the piratical DeVries first among them.

Later that evening, at the height of the wedding feast, Alfar pulled Sander aside.

"Time may not be the same here, Sander, but soon your parents are going to be worried about you," he said simply.

"I know," Sander answered sadly. "We have to leave."

"I've made arrangements with DeVries. He'll sail you down to where Florus Falls empties into the Mauritius. You'll have no trouble finding your way back home along the trail," Alfar said somberly.

"Will I see you again?" Sander asked.

Alfar smiled. "Let's keep a lookout for each other. I'm sure our paths will cross again one day."

Sander fumbled in his pocket and took out the Hessian's match tin. He handed it to Alfar.

"Here. I want you to have this. Something to remember me by."

Alfar took the gift and nodded gratefully.

"Thank you. I have something for you, too. But it's a surprise. It's for the boy who first freed me from the cobwebs of fear. You'll find it soon enough."

Alfar held Sander by the shoulders and looked him in the eye.

"Your father would be proud of you, Sander. And I will never forget you. Now you must go. DeVries is waiting."

Sander gave Alfar a big hug, mumbled his final good-bye, and joined Mini and Bobby, who were standing with DeVries at the head of the trail leading back down the mountain.

They sailed by moonlight. DeVries's sloop cut gently through the water, silver-tipped waves foaming back from her passage. From the broad expanse of the Mauritius, the great bulk of the Dunderburg no longer seemed to brood against the luminous night. A whispering sound came up with the wind.

"Oh, do you feel that breeze?" said Mini.

"It's so warm," Bobby declared.

Sander filled his lungs, inhaling the sweet, scented air of the Highlands.

The warm breeze rose again, filling the canvas. It swept over them, rustling softly like the sound of covers pulled up over a sleeping child.

When Sander got home, it was nearly dawn. As he neared the side porch, he saw a figure rise out of the shadows and come to meet him. It was his father. He held open the screen door as Sander, slightly sheepish, stepped onto the porch. His father took him by the shoulders and looked him in the eye, just as Alfar had done. Sander returned his gaze evenly.

"Everything all right?" his father asked.

"Just fine, Dad. Just fine," Sander answered.

"Good," his father said. "That's good."

He gave his son an enormous bear hug.

"I missed you," he said simply.

Sander could feel his father's warm breath on the back of his neck.

Sander climbed into his bed exhausted and slept like a dead man. He slept right through the thunderstorm that rinsed the Highlands the next morning.

Miles away, on top of the Dunderburg, the

cupped hands of Dwerg's stone statue were raised to the heavens. Rainwater rapidly filled them, and a sparrow dropped down to splash in the improvised birdbath. The bird fluttered its wings, reveling in the rain.

When Sander awoke, he remembered Alfar's final words from the night before. "The cobwebs of fear," he had said. On impulse Sander went straight to his closet and opened the little door into the attic. He found what he was looking for beneath the cobwebs that had trapped the panic-stricken squirrel that night that seemed so long ago. Silverstorm lay gleaming on the wooden floor under the eaves. The magnificent silver belt sparkled in the semi-darkness. Sander picked the belt up lovingly. He laid it in the dresser drawer in his bedroom, hidden beneath his underwear. He heard his father calling him.

"Coming, Dad," he yelled.

Sander grinned to himself and went downstairs to breakfast.